GHOST APPARENT

GHOST APPARENT

JELENA DUNATO

GHOST ORCHID PRESS

Ghost Apparent

First published in Great Britain 2024 by Ghost Orchid Press

ISBN (paperback): 978-1-7390918-5-9

ISBN (hardback): 978-1-7390918-7-3

ISBN (e-book): 978-1-7390918-4-2

Cover illustration © Mia Minnis

Interior illustration © Dory Whynot

For my husband, who never tires of political intrigue.

THE MIRACLE OF THE SEA

The setting sun bleeds into the sea.

Orsiana turns away from the window to face her maid. The girl, armed with pearl-rimmed combs, patiently waits for her to sit down.

"Oh, just braid it, Bria, please," Orsiana says, pulling an unruly lock the colour of bleached sand. Every attempt at coiffure falls apart on her head. "Father won't mind as long as it's neat."

Bria sighs and braids Orsiana's hair so tight it tugs at her scalp painfully. Orsiana winces as the maid wraps the braids in a silver net at the nape of her neck.

This hairstyle is unfashionable and does nothing to improve her looks, but Orsiana doesn't care. The idea that her appearance should draw someone's attention mortifies her. She's not a marble statue, or a doll.

"Has my father sent for me?" she asks.

"Not yet, my lady."

He's late, but that's nothing unusual. Orsiana nods to Bria and slips from her room to a tiny terrace garden, with potted oranges and lemons, fragrant rosemary and sage bushes, and cascades of jasmine pouring down the walls. The long, bright glow of the summer evening lingers in the sky and the stones are still warm to the touch, although the fresh breeze whispering among the leaves already signals the arrival of the night.

The smooth olive wood of the prayer bench is warm under her cheek. She closes her eyes, takes a deep breath. Prayers pour out of her mouth in an easy, practiced rhythm, clearing her mind, opening it to the touch of divine. It comes natural to her, this detachment from the physical world, the feeling that it is just an image painted on a canvas. When she sinks deep enough, she hears the gods murmuring to her.

"Give me strength," she whispers into the gentle breeze, "to make the evening pleasant for my father. To make him happy, just for a little while. He's been carrying his burden for so long. Please, let me make him smile tonight."

Behind this ephemeral world, there is another, where the gods gamble with human lives with terrible indifference. It is a frightening thought, but one that gives Orsiana purpose. If the gods are the only true power, the only eternal truth, what else is there to do but prostrate oneself before them and pray for their help?

"Sweet Lada, let me be charming tonight; gild my drab looks. Cunning Veles, make me witty and amusing. Persistent Korab, give me patience to endure it."

The breeze carries her words into the darkening sky and, as much as she would like to stay and meditate, the burning plum hues of the sunset urge her to move. She rushes through the draughty corridors of the palace towards her father's chambers, over the chequered limestone slabs smoothed down by thousands of tireless feet, under the high arches so finely carved the stone seems lighter than the sea foam. A bored guard waves her through the door into a large room filled with laughter. Her father's usual motley crowd of poets, philosophers, artists, historians, and other brilliant loiterers are scattered around in small groups, vigorously debating.

"My lady Orsiana." A young poet with dark eyes and full, velvety lips brushes her hand as she passes by. "Come help us solve the mystery of the gods. Are they here because we've given human shape to natural forces, or are we here because the gods have dreamed us into being?" His fingers rest on her wrist as he speaks. It's not a caress, but neither is it an accidental touch.

A few months ago, Orsiana was only theoretically aware of the existence of young men, but now the poet's lips distract her, make her wonder at odd, solitary hours of the night what it would be like to kiss them, to bite them, to feel them slide down her body. It's not attraction, she tells herself, just curiosity.

"Later, Master Mareo," she smiles, "I need to speak to my father first."

He feigns disappointment, but his eyes—bright, insolent—stay glued to Orsiana, studying her, *seeing* her. Not just her bare skin under the smooth silk; her pale, lithe limbs; her lap, where the desire pools before dawn like warm honey; but also the thoughts in her head, obscene and shocking, hidden away from everyone, even the gods.

She blushes deeply, turns her head to avoid his gaze, and flees.

Her father's study is big, but every inch of it is filled with eclectic trinkets—books, maps, marble busts, musical and astronomical instruments—not to mention guests engaged in a heated discussion, waving their hands, trying to prove their point. Regaining her composure now that the heat of the poet's body has faded, Orsiana ducks a splash of wine and a chair pushed back, and slips to the other side, where her father presides over his unruly court.

Gospodar Orsolo, the Lord of Abia and the Knez of

Larion, sits next to a young woman, who is showing him the various intricate parts of a mechanical device. His grey eyes are keen and focused, his face kind, and his unruly blond hair even messier than Orsiana's.

"Father." She touches his shoulder, startling him.

"Orsiana." He shoots her a distracted smile. "Come join us. Velissa is explaining how this mechanism works, and it's fascinating. I'm sure there's a spare chair somewhere."

"Father! Have you forgotten?"

"What?" With a wave of his finger, he stops the demonstration and lifts his head to look at Orsiana. She can almost see the scattered, distracted fragments of his mind pulling back together.

"The meeting with Uncle Caril. You promised you'd come."

"Oh no." He rubs the bridge of his nose. "That's today?"

"I'm sure Felino reminded you. And look, you're already dressed for it." Someone has pulled the lord out of his usual bland linens and wools, and dressed him in fine grey silk.

His thumb slides over the intricate silver leaves embroidered on his collar, as if checking if they're real. "I remember now." He rises, drawing several surprised looks and good-natured protests. "Keep going, I'll be back soon," he reassures his guests and holds his elbow out for Orsiana's hand.

In the courtyard of the palace, Orsiana asks, "Do you want a litter?"

He lifts his head towards the clear evening sky, strewn with the first stars. "To Caril's house? No, it's a lovely evening, let's walk."

Torch-lit streets are filled with people going about their business, greeting her father with a quick nod or a wave. They're used to seeing their lord walk among them, and they've known Orsiana since she was a toddler, riding on his shoulders. She feels as safe in the streets as in her own garden.

The mellow atmosphere of the summer evening does not fool her, though; it does not trick her into thinking Abia is a soft-hearted city, a sweet matron with a hug for everyone. On the contrary, she knows Abia is a tight-lipped fisherman's wife with calloused hands, quick to anger and quicker to resentment. It needs a light touch, and respect, and love to submit willingly. It will not be ruled, only stirred gently.

Orsiana lifts her gaze to the open windows on the tall, narrow stone houses, which let the evening breeze in while women lean on the sills or stand on the balconies, chatting with their neighbours. A dark-haired girl with a basket full of immortelle offers her a flower and Orsiana crushes it between her fingers, breathing in its sharp odour.

"I don't look forward to Caril's antics at all," her father says. "I don't know why he insisted on a meeting, today of all days." He pauses in the middle of the street, a flash of his sharp mind cutting briefly through the layers of grief and lethargy. "Orsiana, tell me you didn't plan something."

A pang of shame makes her avoid his gaze. She cannot lie to him. "It's your birthday, father."

"Oh, sweetheart." The rebuke in his words is so gentle she can barely discern it.

Her father never gets angry with her, but neither does he get excited, or scared, or ecstatic or anything else. These days, he moves between mild interest and mild annoyance, and it scares Orsiana. It's just the two of them now, all that's left of their family. She remembers her father as a different man—a man who was happy and involved and enthusiastic, who displayed a full palette of moods, from the most joyous elation to the hottest anger, who knew how to laugh out loud at her jokes or rage at some councillor's wrongdoings. But then Orsiana's mother died, followed by both her brothers, and each death took something out of her father until nought but a shadow was left. He still performs his duties, he still surrounds himself with interesting people, but most days Orsiana feels he's not even there.

And it worries her not just because she doesn't know how to tackle his grief, but also because she's old enough—and perceptive enough—to see that his reclusive ways are threatening his position. Abia's love for its gentle lord is not enough. He needs friends, he needs supporters among his equals, he needs the Great Council at his side and yes, he even needs his ambitious, hungry, extravagance-loving brother.

That's why she forces herself to laugh and say, "It's my duty to rectify your unwillingness to celebrate lavishly. I often fail because I value your peace over our relatives' desire for splendour, but not tonight. Tonight you're going to be surrounded by people who love and support you."

Her father's grief hasn't touched his sharp perception, and that somehow makes it worse. He knows what he should do, he just doesn't have the energy to do it. Orsiana sees a glint of desperate panic on his face. He's a hair's breadth from fleeing.

They are standing in the middle of a busy street, though: the lord, in his beautiful grey silk, and his lovely daughter in her flowing gown. People are starting to stare and soon someone will wonder what's wrong. Her father cannot just turn on his heel and dash into a dark alley like an urchin.

He blinks, and the panic changes into determination. He takes her hand and traps it in the crook of his arm. "Let's do this as quickly as possible and then I can spend the rest of the evening with the people who treat me as their equal, and you can do whatever it is that the girls your age do." He shoots her a side-eyed glance. "Think about young men?"

The quick change of subject takes her unawares. "Men?"

"I've seen that young poet, Mareo, looking at you. I'm not entirely blind, you know. Do you like him?"

"A little." She never lies to her father, and there's no point in hiding so obvious a truth. "But I won't forget my duty, I promise."

She will inherit a vast fortune one day and the stack of suitors' letters grows daily on her father's desk. Her father reads them and puts them aside. He's told Orsiana there's just one suitor in the kingdom worthy of her. Worthy of Abia.

"You'll do your duty one day, but you're too precious to me now." He draws her close and plants a quick kiss on top of her head. "Enjoy your youth while you can. Have your heart broken a little, you'll be wiser for it."

Her father is in a good mood and Orsiana can breathe again. "I'd rather read than have my heart broken, father. I've dug the memoirs of Captain Tregolo from the briny depths of your bookcase."

"Oh, good choice. Have you reached that part with mermaids?"

"Not yet."

"You're going to enjoy it. It's entirely inappropriate for your innocent eyes."

THE VILLA IS an architectural jewel set on a cushion of lush greenery. When Orsiana and her father enter the walled garden, the sounds and scents of the city fall away and the fragrance of the exotic flowers cascading from the branches engulfs them. A long, winding path leads to the front porch. As they walk, the gravel crunches gently beneath their feet and colourful parrots screech their agitated greetings from the tree-tops. They might as well be in some foreign place, an exotic island in the south, where fruit tastes unfamiliar and every bright creature is venomous.

Uncle Caril waits at the foot of the staircase, resplendent in crimson silk like a puffed-up firebird, flanked by his twin sons, the two fair, gangly boys Orsiana can never tell apart. Several distant relatives and a few prominent patricians, the members of her father's Great Council, crowd around them.

"Surprise." Caril opens his arms, welcoming his brother. "Happy birthday."

They embrace, Caril ostentatious, Orsiana's father stiff and puzzled by this display.

Caril then turns to her. "Little Orsiana."

"Uncle." She deftly avoids his hug, for she hates to be touched. She's good at reading people's moods, and Caril's cordiality seems strained, as cloying as his alien plants. "Where is Aunt Roselia? And the girls?"

"Waiting for you inside. Go ahead, we'll follow you in a minute."

She exchanges a brief glance with her father, who shrugs and motions her to go as Caril takes his arm and whispers something in his ear. Six white marble steps lead up to the arched porch with tall, slender columns. Orsiana climbs them slowly, the air before her thick and heavy like syrup. The open door beckons, the bright light and female voices pouring out, but the night tugs at her back. The breeze touches the nape of her neck with its cold fingers like a memory of a bad dream, of frozen earth and deep, dark water.

She shivers. For the first time in her life, the premonition of danger seems absolutely clear, the wrongness of the world obvious.

"Father?" She turns at the top of the stairs, baffled, just in time to see the men gathering around him, the gleam of the first blade slashing through the air and Lord Orsolo collapsing with a cry, blood spurting on the white gravel.

Orsiana screams and the sound slices the night in half, to the possible and impossible, to reality and nightmare. Her legs move by themselves as the men fall on her father like beasts, stabbing, stabbing. The scene is unreal, a rogue shard of broken time, a divine mistake when the gods turned their eyes away and something evil slipped in and took over.

She runs to her father, or she tries to, but rough hands pull her back, and a sweaty palm covers her mouth, cutting off her scream. She kicks her legs in vain, struggling for breath. One of her cousins turns away from her father, staring at her in an intoxicated haze of carnage, his eyes filled with death.

And then it's over; the deed is done and the hands release her. She falls on her father's body, still warm, lying in a widening pool of blood. His eyes are open, his crimson-smeared teeth bared. The beautiful grey silk on his chest is shredded to pieces, soaked in blood, destroyed beyond recognition.

The murderers stand in a silent circle, their blades dripping, their eyes avoiding the scene, like boys caught in mischief. They suddenly seem ashamed and nauseated, breathing through their mouths, their faces tinged green. The metallic stench of slaughter permeates the air.

Orsiana wails like a wounded animal, unable to articulate her pain and horror, unable to call for help or divine justice. The sound is primal, inhuman, and the men back away from her, as if she were the mad, bloodthirsty monster. For a heartbeat, her fury blazes so hot she feels she could grow claws and tear them to ribbons of raw flesh, but then someone pulls a sack over her head, a thick, black velvet cloth that cuts off the light, and chokes her into silence.

~

THE DARKNESS SMELLS of cinnamon and cloves.

Orsiana opens her eyes and finds herself lying on the rough wooden floor of a warehouse lit by a single dark lantern. Her throat hurts and her hands are tied behind her back; she struggles, but is unable to free herself.

"You're awake," her uncle says. He sits in a dim corner; all she can see are his shoes and calves, the crimson fabric sprayed with black blood.

"Where's my father?" she croaks, her voice broken, insecure. Everything around her feels fuzzy and detached, as if all this is happening to someone else. She wants to cry, but she ignores the impulse, pushes it down into the darkness.

"Lord Orsolo was killed by two Seragian assassins who ambushed him in the garden because of a botched trade deal." Caril's tone is calm, matter-of-fact.

"No, that's not—" She stops, while her thoughts move in a sluggish whirl around his words. There were no Seragians in the garden, no strangers at all. Just Caril and his sons and several members of the Great Council.

"The only thing that's still unclear is the destiny of his daughter," Caril continues. "She's believed to be kidnapped by the Seragians."

Orsiana is too shocked to understand. "But I'm here," she says in a small voice.

"You are nowhere at the moment," he tells her in the cold, precise voice of a master addressing a disobeying servant. "Neither safe nor abducted, neither dead nor alive. Your destiny is undecided and it depends entirely on what you do next."

That's too many words for her desperate, grieving brain. When they last spoke—before the murder in the garden, that is—they talked about the food for the celebration, the music, the fireworks. Caril was always the flamboyant uncle, the one prone to excess, the one who enjoyed being wealthy and distinguished. This cold, calculating Caril is a stranger to Orsiana.

"You're just a girl," her uncle says, "too young to understand that your father was unfit to rule. He was on his way to ruin Abia with his lack of concern for our problems, with his refusal to listen to the worried patricians, with his questionable choice of allies. We had to do something." The words in

Caril's mouth reek of envy and cruelty. "Abia needs a strong ruler. Not an indifferent hermit ... or a child."

Orsiana's thoughts collide in a futile attempt to discern what he's saying. This is a coup, that much she understands. And she is a witness, and a threat.

The night outside, the dim vastness of the warehouse and the scuttling of mice under the floorboards emphasize the abnormality.

"What will happen to me?" she asks.

"As I said, it depends on you. If you renounce your claim to Abia, you will be allowed to live in secluded comfort, far from political struggles."

A gilded cage, then. "And if I don't?"

Uncle Caril approaches her and kneels on the floor. The light reveals the expression of incredulity on his face as he bends down so close his breath touches her cheek. "What else can you do? You're just a girl—you have no allies, no power, no soldiers."

This slip into ugliness is liberating, for it shatters the illusion of polite lunacy.

"Be reasonable, Orsiana," he continues. "The city belongs to me now and there's nothing you can do about it. Your refusal will bring you nothing but harm."

Orsiana closes her eyes. A secluded cottage somewhere where she could grieve in peace, with no one to bother her, no one to demand her attention—where she could slowly fade to nothingness—seems attractive. And yet, a tiny, inflexible part of her soul refuses to bend, rejects reasonable arguments.

"I am the last remaining child of Gospodar Orsolo of Abia. I am his heiress. I can't pretend to be someone else," she says. It's the unwise answer, the dangerous answer, the lethal answer. Yet everything else would be a betrayal of her father, her whole family. She cannot step away from who she is; she'd rather die as Orsiana than live as some nameless shadow.

Her uncle snorts. "Brave words from a little girl. You're just as reckless as he was." He gags her with a scarf and throws a velvet sack over her head. "I gave you a chance to live a gentle life," he whispers in her ear, tearing her silk dress off her, leaving her in a linen chemise. "Remember you chose this."

Panic chokes Orsiana as he drags her out of the warehouse, throws her in a wagon, and covers her with rough sackcloth. There is a murmur of voices, but she cannot make out the words, drowned out by the cries of the gulls and the soft lapping of the waves as a pair of hands grab her and throw her into a boat.

She curls up on a wet fishing net in the bottom and it occurs to her that Uncle Caril is making her disappear. No one has seen her leaving his villa, or board this boat. No one but him will know what happened to her.

She feverishly considers the options. The fisherman's boat is small, it can't take them very far. There are few probable destinations: lighthouse on the Gull Island, one of the tiny villages along the coast or the bottom of the bay. She wriggles, trying to loosen the stiff, itchy rope binding her wrists.

"Don't fuss." A foot meets her ribs in a vile prod, making her yelp. It's a sharp warning that she's not the lord's daughter anymore, but a nameless girl, a package to be delivered. There's nothing for her to do but lie still and ignore the numbness of her arms and the cold that seeps into her bones while the oars move in a slow rhythm and the boat cuts through the waves.

Orsiana smells it before she hears it, before the boat slows down or the fisherman calls the crew. The stink hits her like a fist and she can't escape it, she must breathe it in, terrified it will make her retch and choke on her own vomit because her mouth is gagged.

She's never smelt it before, but there's no ambiguity: nothing in the world reeks like a slaver. The odour of desperation and fear; of human filth; of shit, piss and vomit; of bodies crammed together in the hold, stewing in squalid brine.

Seragian slavers are not permitted to enter the port of Abia, but sometimes they anchor in the bay, and Abian merchants sell them water and food. It is easy to guess that Uncle Caril is one of those merchants, but this time he's sending something far more precious than a barrel of salt fish or a dozen sacks of cabbage. There are no passengers aboard the slavers, for no free souls would ever choose to travel in that manner. Orsiana is cargo.

The man pulls the oars in, and she can hear a sailor yell, "Who goes there?"

There is no time to think, no way to bargain or plead. If the only choice is between slavery and death, then it is no choice at all.

She pushes herself up, feeling the curve of the hull. The small boat rocks wildly, the fisherman shouts, but before he can stop her, she steps on the gunwale and jumps.

Cold water shocks her. She cannot swim with her hands tied behind her back. The waves close above her head and the depths suck her in. She has no plan, no hope of escape; there's barely enough time to send a quick, desperate prayer to the God of the Sea. *Ever-changing Korab, receive my soul. Have mercy on me.*

She hears a splash as a body dives after her and the fisherman grabs her. She cannot fight, but she thinks, *My body is made of lead, and it sinks and sinks and sinks.*

The grip loosens, the hands let go. She plunges like a stone, the pressure building up in her ears, squeezing the last bubbles of air out of her lungs. The water turns very cold and dark, and eerily silent. She doesn't want to struggle, but her body does it anyway, desperate for a breath of air, filled with an unrelenting wish for life.

With every morsel of her self-control, she fights the urge to breathe in, but her terror-stricken body disobeys. Her lungs fill with black water, and she drowns.

～

SOMEONE PULLS the hood off her head. A flash of green light in the darkness, and the scarf that gagged her disappears. She opens her mouth, but instead of water rushing in, another mouth covers hers. Cold tongue slides between her lips, a taste of fish and brine, a hint of sharp teeth. Her lungs expand and she realizes she's breathing at the bottom of the sea.

A luminescent creature swims around her in the dark and a shocking realization hits Orsiana that it must be a sea maiden. It doesn't resemble the seductive girls from Captain Tregolo's stories, and yet it possesses a unique, astonishing beauty. Its face looks nothing like a human face, its skin greenish and glowing, stretched over sharp bones; its eyes enormous; its mouth wide and filled with sharp teeth. A blue cloud of long, hair-thin feelers surrounds its head like an eerie frame. The creature has a gilled neck, a delicately scaled torso, and two arms, but there's no trace of breasts sailors like to describe. (*Of course,* Orsiana thinks, *what would be their purpose?*) The torso seamlessly melts into a long, iridescent tail.

Orsiana stares in awe as the creature beckons with its webbed fingers. There are no words but the command to follow is clear and Orsiana obeys, walking on the white sand, raising small clouds where her feet touch it. The sea maiden's luminescence is the only light she has, and it reveals very little: the sand beneath her feet, the few curious fish brave enough to come close. Orsiana cannot say how deep she is or how long she walks before she falls into a trance, emptying her head of everything but the rhythm of her footsteps.

The precipice appears so suddenly Orsiana almost plunges

over it. She stops at the last moment, waving her hands in panic, pushing herself backwards through the dark water.

A seemingly endless black crevice runs across the sea bed and although Orsiana doesn't know how deep she is now, she knows the crevice is infinitely deeper, so deep it might as well be bottomless. A primal fear of the sea, of the depths no human eye has ever seen, freezes her legs. She shakes her head in mute terror, signalling to the creature that she cannot go forward.

The sea maiden moves her shoulders in a manner that can only be interpreted as a shrug and points at their surroundings: the sand, the darkness, the impenetrable mass of water above their heads, as if saying, *What else is there to do?* Orsiana can go forth or remain here forever, a bleached skeleton on the white sand.

The fear is a physical thing; it shakes her body and grips her throat with its sharp claws and she wrestles it unsuccessfully for a while, trying to push it down, make it disappear. It's stronger than her, it doesn't let go. Desperate, Orsiana prepares to explain to the sea maiden that she is too afraid, when the sound of her father's voice echoes in her head.

"It's just fear, Orsiana." A memory of Lord Orsolo teaching her to ride, her head barely reaching his belt and the brown mare towering over both of them, rolling her eyes impatiently. "A warning, not a command. Acknowledge it, then do what you must."

She ceases fighting. The fear blooms inside her chest like ink stains in water and she welcomes it. It's huge and powerful. She takes the sea maiden's hand, closes her eyes and steps over the precipice.

They dive fast, the sea maiden pulling her down, Orsiana keeping her eyes firmly shut to prevent them from seeing the empty darkness that surrounds them. The water turns so cold it sucks every last bit of warmth out of Orsiana's body. She might as well be a fish now, cold-blooded and slippery.

Then light touches Orsiana's eyelids—not the cold luminescence of the sea maiden, but a bright, golden glow, and she opens her eyes. A magnificent scene startles her: an enormous palace of bleached bones, mother-of-pearl, and coral rises from the golden sand, shining like a solitary star. Towers spiral up like gargantuan snail shells above their heads as they step through a majestic shark jaw into a hall. Orsiana's eyes marvel at the glimmering walls and sea-star studded ceiling, held up by the ribs of a whale. Other sea creatures swim around, colourful fish and sea maidens and ghostly jellyfish, but no one tries to stop them as they approach the throne: a golden boat wedged between two noble pen shells, as tall as Orsiana.

A man sits in the boat, or at least a creature resembling a human, with nothing fish-like about him. He is young and beautiful, with long golden-brown hair and beard and a strong body. In his right hand he holds a trident. When his eyes meet Orsiana's, she sees the golden whirl of stars and the eternal blackness between them and falls to her knees, certain that she is in a presence of a god.

"Little Orsiana, you pray so loudly your words reach the deepest trenches of the sea," the god's voice booms in her head.

"I'm sorry, o mighty, ever-changing Korab," she replies, prostrate before him. "I cried in desperation, I didn't mean to disturb you."

Her body shakes so badly the sand around her moves.

"Lift your head, let me see you." The god's eerie eyes study her face. "You called me and I answered. Tell me what you wish for."

Confusion muddles Orsiana's thoughts. All her solitary hours of prayer did nothing to prepare her for this. She never dared to hope that the gods heard her prayers, let alone wished to answer them. Like a mayfly, like a blink of an eye, her life must be an insignificant flash of light to them. She is nothing, a grain of sand on the ocean floor. And yet ...

What *does* she want?

Images rush through her mind: blades glowing, her father falling down, blood on the gravel. She wants that evening to disappear; she wishes it had never happened. She wants her father back.

Pain racks her chest as she lifts her face to the god. She realizes she hasn't said a word, and yet, Korab has heard her thoughts clearly. A brief spark of pity flashes in his eyes.

"That's impossible." Korab shakes his majestic head. "I cannot undo things or change the course of past events, and I cannot send you back because humans cannot travel in time."

Orsiana nods in mute understanding, her heart sinking. If it's impossible to change what happened, than what's the point of prayers and gods?

She's thinking too loudly, obviously, because Korab frowns. "I might decide to keep you here, with my creatures. You're not pretty enough to be an ornament, but some might find you interesting."

For a brief moment, an eternity at the bottom of the sea seems like an easy escape. There's nothing left for her on the surface but death and grief. Even the gods cannot erase that. Her father is dead, and Caril has seized Abia with his bloody claws.

Abia, she still has Abia.

"Don't keep me here, please." There's some fire left in her, after all. "I want to go back to the surface, I want to go home to Abia."

"And what are you willing to pay for it?"

"Pay?" Orsiana's eyes slide to her white shift, her bare feet. "I have noth—"

"Really, girl, why do you invoke gods if you're not

prepared to bargain?" Korab frowns. "I'll grant your wish and take that piercing voice of yours in return. I'll let my sea maidens use it to lure sailors, and we'll finally have some amusement here. Do we have a deal?"

"Yes," Orsiana agrees, "but how—"

Korab flicks his fingers and the audience is over. The sea maiden grabs Orsiana's hand and pulls her up, through the whale ribs, beside spiral towers, through the black water, out of the trench and towards the surface.

WHEN THE SEA maiden leaves her on a pebbled beach, it's already dawn. Wet and shivering, Orsiana hides from the fishermen going out to sea and then runs into the small fishing village, already waking up. She peeks through a crack in a wooden shutter and sees a young woman nursing a baby on a low pallet. Too shy to disturb her and too embarrassed to barter, she grabs a rough homespun tunic off a washing line and leaves her fine linen shift in its place, hoping that the woman will find a use for it, perhaps wrap her newborn in its soft fabric.

There are no shoes or sandals to be pilfered, so Orsiana sets off towards Abia barefooted. Her soles are soft, used to walking on woollen carpets, not the hard, rocky surface of the road. Abia is less than half a mile away, but by the time she reaches the gate, her feet are bleeding. The warmth of her body releases the odours the tunic is permeated with, and she arrives to her own city stinking of sweat and fish. Not a single guard turns in her direction; she's just a poor, filthy girl.

Her first impulse is to run home, to the palace. Everything she has—everything she is—is still tucked in there. Her clothes, her books, her mother's jewellery, her father's collection of curiosities. And the people who've known her since the day she was born: her maids, the servants, the cooks, the grooms—a small universe she belongs to. If she could just reach it, she could become herself again and find the strength to face the world.

But when she approaches the palace, she sees that every entrance, even the ones meant for servants, is swarmed with men in Caril's black and silver livery. The dream-like architecture, the white stone lace, the tall, pointed arches, the elegant spiral columns suddenly don't look so playful and enchanting, but aloof and foreboding.

Orsiana joins a line of washerwomen at a back entrance and keeps her head down, hoping to find out what's going on. The guards Orsiana doesn't recognize search every woman and a clerk takes down their names.

"What's going on? Why are you doing this?" the women ask.

"It's the new lord's orders," the clerk replies. "Gospodar Caril wants to know who enters his palace and what they do there."

Gospodar Caril? Orsiana gags just as a heavy hand lands on her shoulder. "You're no washerwoman," a guard says. "What are you doing here?"

She opens her mouth to reply, but her brain freezes. She knows every job in the palace a young woman could do, she could list them in her sleep, yet no words cross her lips.

"We don't need beggars." The guard pushes her so hard she stumbles and lands on her backside. "Get lost."

Several women glance at Orsiana sprawled in the dust and quickly avert their eyes in silence. Their jobs are more important than some scruffy girl. Cheeks burning with humiliation, Orsiana scrambles up and escapes into one of the side alleys.

She cannot go home.

With her back pressed against the wall, she lifts her head, watching the roofs of the palace towering over the neighbouring buildings. So close, so unattainable. Breathing slowly, she tries to swallow her tears, but they keep coming in a warm flood, leaving salty rivulets on her cheeks, dripping on her stained tunic.

Stupid, ignorant Orsiana. What did she think, that she would just walk into the palace, that nothing has changed since yesterday? The whole world has changed. And now there's no place for her in it.

A woman walking down the alley with a basket over her arm glances at Orsiana, pauses, takes a piece of rye bread out of the basket, and pushes it into her hand without a word. For a heartbeat, Orsiana thinks the woman has recognized her, that her gift is a gesture of support, but then it dawns on her that she looks like a beggar. The woman disappears before Orsiana can thank her. The bread is dark and heavy, with a grainy texture. Although she's seen nothing but white rolls at her father's table, her stomach painfully reminds her that she's eaten nothing for a very long time, and she devours the bread in a few bites.

Her stomach appeased, Orsiana moves away from the palace with a heavy heart and roams the streets, unsure what to do next. A strange atmosphere engulfs the city like a suffocating fog. The taverns are ominously quiet, devoid of music and laughter. People sit in small groups, whispering among themselves, falling silent the moment a stranger approaches them. Street vendors call their wares, but don't chat with their customers, don't smile as they wrap their parcels or hand over the hot food. Even the fishmongers refrain from gossiping, gutting the fish in silence, their blades scraping the silvery scales in short, precise movements. Orsiana hears her father's name whispered a few times, but when she looks for the person speaking it, no one wants to meet her eyes. Citizens are filled with confusion, doubt and, above all, fear.

My father was murdered, she wants to shout, to share her

grief with them. They wouldn't recognize her, though, filthy and ragged as she is. And even if they did, what could they do? Storm the palace with their knives and cudgels, grab Caril by the scruff of his neck and throw him out? She'd love to see that, but it's a silly dream, not a battle plan.

She needs help from someone clever and powerful, someone who is not afraid to stand up to Caril.

Orsiana pauses on a street corner and considers her possible allies. She recalls the men she's seen dining with her father in the last few months, the ones he considered his friends, the ones he visited or hunted with. The ones who treated her kindly and with respect.

One name pops up. Gospodar Irlin, the companion her father grew up with, his cousin and friend. If anyone is able to help her, it's him. He has enough money, and men, and friends to protect her when she tells her story. Safe in his house, she could rally the faithful nobles, and demand justice.

Two hundred paces west from the main square, the back entrance to Gospodar Irlin's house sits on a busy street and, unlike the palace, there are no guards at the door. Young men delivering goods and serving girls running about their chores dash in and out, and nobody pays attention to a small girl slipping in. Orsiana rushes through the servants' quarters, finds the back stairs leading to the upper floor. Avoiding the busy maids and handsy grooms, she takes a moment to recall the layout of the house, and then runs to the study. She knocks on the heavy wooden door, praying that her father's friend is there.

"Come in," a voice says.

She opens the door and slips in. The man sitting at the desk is her father's age, but unlike Lord Orsolo, he's dark and stocky, with greying black hair. Clean shaven and clad in simple linens, he looks more like a modest merchant than a rich patrician. When he lifts his head, a confused frown creases his brow before his eyes widen. "Little Orsiana? Is that you?"

She crosses the soft carpet, her heart filled with relief, and opens her mouth to answer. No sound comes out, not even a whisper. She tries again, thinking that she swallowed too much seawater, or that her throat is still too raw from the hard grip that choked her senseless, but no matter how she tries, her mouth refuses to shape words. Instead, she yawns like a fish on a pier, choking.

"Oh, you poor girl! I can't imagine the ordeal!" Gospodar Irlin rushes to her and leads her to a chair. "We were all shocked when we heard the news this morning. I'm so sorry, I loved Orsolo like a brother. It's terrible, terrible!"

She still can't speak. Instead, she hangs on his arm, looking up into his eyes, and the pain and pity she sees there break a dam inside her, and all the shock, terror, and grief pour out in a flood of silent, bitter tears. Lord Irlin holds her like a child, stroking her hair and murmuring, "There, there. "

She cries for a long time, until her face bloats and her nose is clogged and her chest hurts from sobbing. It feels like all the salt water she has swallowed now must flow out of her, drenching her clothes and leaving dark stains on the colourful carpet.

"You're safe now, child. The worst is over." Gospodar Irlin hands her a clean handkerchief and watches her closely while she wipes her face, taking in her matted hair, her dirty tunic, and bleeding feet. "Did they hurt you?"

The question seems absurd, of course they hurt her, but then she notices him looking at her bare, bruised legs and realization shocks her. She shakes her head quickly, blushing. No, they didn't hurt her like that. Caril is a beast, but not *that* kind of beast.

"And your voice ... is it an injury, or shock, or something else?"

She shakes her head in confusion, struggling to follow the conversation.

"I've heard that extreme distress can do that." He frowns. "The important thing is that you're alive and safe. Let's get you bathed, and find you some decent clothes. And then some food, perhaps?"

She nods.

He calls his servants, gives them instructions. And then, just as she's leaving his study, following a maid and looking forward to a warm bath, he says, "I'll send a message to Caril right away. He'll be relieved to know that you're safe."

She turns back, dismayed, panic seizing her chest, and then runs across the room. Unable to scream that it's the worst possible thing he can do to her, she grabs his arm, digging her fingers into his flesh, shaking her head violently, trying to make him understand.

He stares at her in confusion, removing her hand gently, but firmly. "He's mad with worry. He thought those Seragian assassins who killed your father abducted you."

The surprise and shock on her face make him pause.

"You didn't know it was the Seragians? Of course, how stupid of me," he exclaims. "I suppose it was all too sudden for you to understand, a brief ordeal in the dark." He shakes his head and she recognizes genuine—if mistaken—grief on his face. "It was two Seragian assassins who attacked your father, probably because a month ago he once again refused to let the Seragian slavers enter the port. They're still on the run, but there are witnesses who saw them following you to Caril's house, and then fleeing the garden later. They will surely be caught soon. When Caril and the others found your father alone, stabbed to death, they were convinced the Seragians must have abducted you. But you escaped, didn't you?"

She doubts her own memory for a moment; the previous day was a sequence of incomprehensible events she doesn't want to think about. It would be a relief to agree with Gospodar Irlin, to blame the Seragians—the two evil, faceless criminals—for her father's death.

But that's exactly what Caril wants. He mentioned the Seragians in the warehouse. He chose the culprits wisely. Despite some merchants and nobles in Abia, including Caril, trading with those horrendous vessels, the city is not too keen on the imperial tradition of slavery, especially knowing that the Seragians always look for an opportunity to enlarge their vast empire.

Orsiana is certain now that her uncle didn't come up with that lie on the spot. It was all planned, a premeditated political assassination. His sons, the members of the Great Council who participated in her father's murder: they must have all agreed. Caril now has witnesses to confirm his story. Of course he does.

They butchered her father because the way he ruled Abia didn't suit their interests.

She reaches for the quill on his desk and dips it in ink. There's no paper, but she opens a random book and scribbles in the margin, "Caril killed my father", underlining it twice, splattering ink all over the page. She lifts it and shows it to Gospodar Irlin, her grip so hard her fingers turn white.

His eyes fly over the words and time slows down, the moment stretching enough to let her see first the surprise, then the incredulity and finally the denial on his face. Orsiana's heart sinks. The truth she's revealing is too hard to swallow, too uncomfortable, too dangerous. Caril sits in the palace, surrounded by his supporters, spreading his cleverly shaped lies. And she is just a desperate, grieving girl spewing fatal nonsense.

Lord Irlin's eyes fill with pity once again, but this time it feels condescending and insincere. He pulls the book out of her grasp and tears the offending page out, crumpling it in his large hand. "You must be confused by the shock, my dear," he says, his voice quavering. "Many people saw what happened."

She shakes her head violently and tries to rip the page out of his hand as if it were some kind of undeniable proof, but he's too strong for her. His fingers close like steel shackles around her wrists. She trashes madly, but the more she resists, the firmer his hold becomes.

"Orsiana, please, you'll hurt yourself."

The maid, still standing at the door and watching the whole ordeal, steps hesitantly towards them. "My lord, what—"

"Get help," he barks.

Orsiana fights with every morsel of strength, certain that if Caril catches her, she'll disappear for real this time, never to come back. Her elbow connects with Lord Irlin's plexus and his grip relaxes for a moment. She runs, but two brawny servants block the door. They grab her by the arms and lift her unceremoniously.

"Shall we throw this wild cat out, my lord?" one of them asks.

"No, carry her to the third floor."

They drag her to the servants' quarters, high in the attic, into a small chamber with a window too narrow for escape. No bath, no new clothes, no food is waiting for her. When they lock her in, she checks every wall, every floorboard, every slanting beam in a desperate search for a way out, but the room is as secure as a prison cell.

Realizing there's no escape, Orsiana kneels on the hard floor, takes a deep breath, and closes her eyes. Tears escape the silken barrier of her lashes and roll down her cheeks. *I don't know what to do*, she tells the gods in the hopeless darkness that fills her head. *Korab has given me a chance to get my life back, but I'm not clever enough to use it. Please, please show me what to do. Cunning Veles, lord of tricks and deceit, help me escape this trap. Show me what to do.*

Nothing happens. She cannot feel the connection to the divine; there's no eternity behind these thin, whitewashed walls, no burning stars above her head. There's just this bleak room she is trapped in, and futile, whining thoughts rushing through her head.

Caril has moved fast, she realizes now. He seized the palace and probably proclaimed himself the ruler of the city, despite the fact he needs the approval of the Council and the king to do that. If the councillors believe Gospodar Orsolo and his daughter are dead, then they won't even recognize this as a coup. Caril is the next in line, the rightful heir to Abia.

Without the immediate Seragian threat, the patricians would drag their feet as usual, insisting that the Council obey Abia's laws and traditions with correctness that borders on pettiness. They would seek the proof of their lord's unexpected demise, search for eye-witnesses to support Caril's story; they would demand to examine the bodies of the victims and see the assassins brought to justice first.

But Caril is cunning. The perceived Seragian blade at Abia's throat will force the Council to act. The patricians will want a new ruler fast. And Orsiana is locked in an attic, unable to prove that she's alive, with Caril on his way to remove her. She won't get a chance to slip away this time.

Everything her father has taught her, all the history lessons, all the treatises on ruling she read, it was all in vain. She walked right into a trap, like a naïve child who'll never be fit to rule Abia.

Of course the gods won't listen to her prayers. She managed to squander Korab's gift in less than a day. She'll lose Abia and her life because she is a failure, a stupid girl unworthy of her father's legacy.

She's still berating herself when floorboards in the corridor outside creak, announcing visitors. Lord Irlin unlocks the door and marches in with a tall, black-clad physician she's never seen before.

"... raving and delusional," Lord Irlin says on the doorstep.

Orsiana freezes and looks into the physician's eyes. Her reflection tells her she'll find no ally in him. What he sees is a picture of madness: a bruised, dishevelled, frantic, half-naked girl, mute and gesticulating wildly.

Pure despair makes her dash for the door, but she barely makes three steps before the physician grabs her. "Not so fast," he says. He presses an acrid-smelling rag over her nose and mouth. She holds her breath for as long as she can, but the urge to breathe is stronger than her will. She inhales and the room around her loses its edges and melts into darkness.

2

THE MIRACLE OF DECEIT

Orsiana opens her eyes in a vast cavern, stalactites hanging above her head like dragon's teeth, yellowish and lethally sharp. Water drips somewhere in the distance, chopping time into perfect intervals; the only moving element in the stale, cold interior. The cavern is not dark: an invisible source of light bathes it in a soft golden glow, and when her eyes adapt, she sees dots of vividly coloured glass reflecting the light. No, not glass—gems. Emeralds, amethysts, sapphires, and rubies, glowing like multi-coloured embers.

The scene has a dreamlike quality, weirdly clear and outlandish at the same time, but just like Korab's castle under the sea, Orsiana knows this cavern is real, or as real as anything that the gods dream into being can be.

She gets up, disoriented. There is no path, no visible exit, nothing to guide her. A slight difference in the intensity of light suggests there might be a source somewhere, so she walks towards it, circling around the stalagmites shooting up, her feet bare on the cold rock.

Time stretches unpredictably; she feels neither hunger nor

thirst, but the cold gradually seeps into her bones and makes her shiver. She walks through the landscape that looks so uniform she cannot orientate herself. The light gradually grows stronger, giving her hope she's moving in the right direction.

As she passes through a strange portal-like rock formation, the light becomes stronger still, the glare blinding her, forcing her to peer through her eyelashes. A coil of liquid gold untangles before her.

"Little Orsiana," a voice says and an eye opens among the waves of gold, as big as her head, bright yellow with a slit black pupil. A snake's eye.

She stands before it, a terrified rabbit frozen with fear.

The enormous snake moves with a sound as smooth as satin sliding off a rack, until its head, as large as an ox, almost touches Orsiana. "What are you doing here?" the god asks.

Despite praying for help in the attic room, Orsiana is just as stunned as when she met Korab. Being plucked out of the human realm and thrown before a deity is not an event one can prepare for in advance.

"O, cunning Veles, the cleverest of gods ... I don't know," Orsiana answers in her head, her voice still gone. "I was praying for an escape, and then—"

The liquid blaze of the god's eye burns her like the sun. "I'm not asking how you got here, I know that. You're here because your shrieking woke me up, because you're falling through the layers of time, tearing them and leaving a hole that hurts like a knife-wound. Every god hears you now, but I was the closest. So, tell me, what are you doing here? What do you want?"

This time, Orsiana is better prepared. "I come to you seeking help," she pleads.

Veles hisses softly and stares at her with his unblinking eye. "I am hungry," his voice echoes inside her skull, "and you look deliciously tender. Should I eat you or should I hear you out?"

Her body trembles but she meets his gaze directly. "I'm all bones, o mighty Veles, you wouldn't find me tasty."

The god scoffs. "You're a funny little thing. Tell me what you want."

"I would like my voice back." There are many things Orsiana wants, but she's learning quickly that it's best to be short and precise with the gods. And perhaps not too greedy, or the price might be too steep.

"And why do you need your voice back? You shriek loud enough without it." A forked tongue flickers out of the god's mouth and disappears again.

"I need my voice to tell people what happened."

"Why?"

"So I can avenge my father's death."

The great coil rolls towards her like a golden tide. "Is that what you plan to do? Run around and cry murder until someone sticks a knife in you and makes you shut up?"

A pang of fury prods at her chest, but she's still collected enough to know it would be unwise to quarrel with a god. "I —no, I'm not going to do that. I will be careful."

"And do what?"

"I don't know yet!" She balls her fists in exasperation. "Why does it matter to you anyway? I am just one powerless girl. What difference does it make to you if I succeed or fail?"

"It makes all the difference in the world, little Orsiana," the great eye blinks slowly, "whether you rule Abia or your uncle does."

She should ask what it means, she really should. The great eye stares in expectation, reading her thoughts, waiting for her to form a question. But she doesn't want to know. Even the perfectly ordinary, human part of the story is too vast for her to handle. She cannot face some divine prophecy, some additional burden on her skinny shoulders. She can barely take care of herself, let alone the divine plans.

"I like you," the god chuckles. "You don't think you're special, like some people."

Orsiana nods, although she has no idea what Veles is talking about. The more they talk, the more confused she gets. She tries to clear her foggy thoughts and hang on to the one important thing. "Can I have my voice back?" she pleads again.

The god hisses softly. "I can grant you that. But first, let me see if you're clever enough to deserve it. Let's play a little game. Do you like riddles?"

Orsiana doesn't like riddles, but Veles is a trickster god, and she understands what he wants. She nods.

"Fine. If you solve it, I'll grant you your wish. If you don't —" A forked tongue shoots out of his mouth and stops a hair's breadth from her face before disappearing again.

She flinches but resists the urge to run. "I'm ready."

"All right, here's my riddle: what can you keep only if you give it to someone else?"

Like all riddles, it seems frustratingly vague and oddly specific. Various answers shoot through her mind. What can one give to someone else? Happiness, friendship, love. But that's all too imprecise, and far from something a god of deceit would appreciate. She thinks about things one can keep: grudges, oaths, promises. She has a long list of those, but none fit.

"Do you know the answer?" Veles asks.

Orsiana feverishly tests the expressions in her mind. *I'll give you my ... what? I'll keep my ...*

"Time's up," Veles says.

Orsiana bites her lip. "My word," she says aloud, her voice her own once again. She exclaims and falls to her knees before the giant snake. "Thank you!"

Veles hisses. "That was obvious, wasn't it?" The yellow eye reflects Orsiana's image, its curve twisting it into a strange shape. "Just as you will be obvious when you wake up, a little girl shouting her pain for all the world to hear. That won't do." The tongue flickers again, fast as lightning. "I'll give you another gift beside your voice, just to make things more interesting. You might find it useful."

Orsiana's mind writhes in panic. "O lord of tricksters, please don't—"

∽

ORSIANA WAKES with a start just as the door to her tiny attic room opens and Gospodar Irlin steps in, followed by her uncle. She doesn't give any sign she's awake, curled under the covers like a terrified mouse in the presence of hungry cats.

"She's very fragile, physically and mentally," her host says, while Caril nods, his face a perfect image of loving worry.

Dressed in sombre ash-grey silk, free of his customary frippery, her uncle looks like a fresher, plumper version of his late brother. The resemblance is too striking to be a coincidence.

"No serious wounds, but extreme exhaustion, shock, and confusion," Gospodar Irlin continues. "She couldn't speak, but she wrote down wild things about the murder. She didn't know anything about the Seragian assassins. She thought you were responsible for Orsolo's death."

"The poor child must be out of her mind," Caril cuts him off. "And the least we say about it, the better." He shakes his head. "The very thought that I would hurt my brother ... it's monstrous. Don't mention it to anyone, don't even think about it. You know how the rumours fly."

"Of course." Lord Irlin nods, an obedient puppet. Is it possible that he doesn't see through Caril's mask, through his lies, or did he simply decide to bet on the strongest player? "I destroyed her writing immediately. No one knows about it."

Neither Irlin nor Caril are brawny men, one short and round, the other fine-boned and overindulged. But to Orsiana, peeking from under the covers, they seem like giants, their heads reaching to the slanted ceiling, their bodies taking up all the space. There's no slipping past them, no dodging them.

The dream of the snake is vivid in her head. *What do you want?* he asked. She wants to tell the truth, but this is not the time to test her regained voice. She lies still, peering through her eyelashes, pretending to be asleep. Perhaps Caril won't snatch her right away if she's too weak to get up. As long as she's in Lord Irlin's house, she won't disappear or get murdered in some corner.

"Little Orsiana, are you awake?" Caril says, gently pulling the cover away from her face. Then he gasps. "What is this?" His tone turns unpleasant.

"What?" Irlin asks. "Oh." He stares at the key in his hand then turns around the room in confusion. "This is the right room, but—"

"I don't know what sick game you're playing, but this is not my niece," Caril barks. "Even a fool like you should be able to see that."

"I assure you, she was—"

Hard fingers sink into Orsiana's shoulder and Caril shakes her. "Wake up, whelp. Where is Orsiana?"

As she opens her eyes and sits up, she doesn't have to feign confusion because she's just as baffled as the two men. "My lords?" She rubs her eyes and notices her hands. They're the colour of polished olive wood. The tresses falling down her shoulders are dark brown. *Make things more interesting*, the trickster god had said.

"Who are you and where is Orsiana?" Lord Irlin asks.

She doesn't look like herself, that's obvious. She's just a

random girl in a servant's room, and suddenly she understands the gift Veles has given her. "I'm Bria, my lord, a kitchen maid." Orsiana would bet that Lord Irlin has no idea who washes his pots. "I was working this morning, but then I got the flux and fever and the cook sent me up here—"

It works like magic; they both retreat to the door as fast as they can.

"Guards!" Caril calls, and then turns to Irlin, seething. "I will have this house searched from the basement to the rafters. If my niece is not here—"

"I promise you, she came to me for help, terribly distressed, unable to speak."

Both men leave the room shouting, without as much as a glance towards Orsiana. As soon as the voices disappear down the corridor, she lets out a sigh of relief. She's safe for the moment, but she cannot stay in this house. Even if the lord doesn't know who works in his kitchen, the cook and the maids surely do. Soon they will realize she's an intruder.

But the Trickster God's ruse has done something to her brain, too. A spark of daring glows in the darkness of her mind, a speck of reckless courage that compels her to search the other rooms in the attic, opening the simple wooden chests until she finds a threadbare linen shift, a sober brown dress with frayed hems, and a pair of worn-out sandals that fit her small feet.

A fragment of a broken mirror on a window sill draws her attention. Her new face is plain, unmemorable. With dark eyes, snub nose, and a spattering of pimples on her forehead, she looks just like any other adolescent girl in Abia.

She descends the servants' stairs as Caril's guards turn the house upside down, looking for a pale, fair-haired girl who doesn't exist anymore, and for the tiniest fraction of a heartbeat, Veles' trick makes her smile. The lord's study is empty as she passes by, and feeling impossibly sly, she dashes in, searches through the drawers, and pockets a handful of coins, silver and gold. She's a thief now, but it doesn't bother her nearly as much as she expected it would. After all, Bria the maid is not above nicking a coin or two if the opportunity presents itself. What is a fistful of silver compared with the whole city Caril stole from her?

Then she steps out of the house and into the morning crowd. It's the second day since her father's murder and the summer sky above Abia is bright blue. The mood in the streets is darker than winter storm clouds, though, and just as ominously subdued as when she walked them the day before. Her father has taught her to look at people, to read their faces, to listen to the murmur of the crowd. And the crowd in the markets of Abia, in the taverns, on the piers, writhes in confusion and grief. The news of Lord Orsolo's death has spread, along with the rumour that he was assassinated by the Seragian slave masters for refusing to let their ships enter the port. It's a plausible enough theory—the Seragians have always played dirty, and they have never been friends of Abia. But the perpetrators have not been caught, there is nowhere for the crowd to direct their anger, and the city government is currently headless. No one mentions Caril and his takeover of the palace; the streets show no interest or support for him.

Abia is a prize, waiting to be snatched, its destiny a coin spinning in the air.

Orsiana runs down to the sea and scrambles atop the harbour wall, ignoring the sharp, salty wind, and sits on the warm stones, facing the city. The large port is filled with movement, the merchant vessels rocking gently and small boats dashing between them. Huge warehouses swallow or spew out bales of fabric, barrels of salt fish and wine, sacks of wheat. The crowded, winding streets lead away from the port, lined by the endless rows of narrow stone houses crooked like a beggar's teeth. The immense bulk of the palace and the dizzy open space of the square before it blind the eye with their whiteness. Rows upon rows of red roofs, encircled within the massive city walls, crowd together like roosting chickens.

She knows that the gift of the trickster god is not only meant to confuse other people, it's meant to confuse her too. No god's gift is ever straightforward or entirely good, and Veles infused his trick with a dilemma. He has given her the freedom to walk away from everything. She has a new face; she could have a new life, a destiny without duty and inherited obligations. She could survive on her skills only—she could teach writing, or history, or music; she could devote her life to gods who seem to hear her when she prays, and become a priestess. She could go anywhere, be anything.

It would be a lie to say she has never thought about it. Being born into a family like hers meant she had very little choice. The death of her brothers and her father's refusal to marry again locked her in the position of the heiress to Abia and the whole province of Larion. No one has ever asked if she wanted it.

When she became old enough to understand the burden, she grew angry with her father, with her destiny. She rebelled, in her own quiet way. She shunned her public duties, refused her private ones; she retreated into solitude, devoted her time to meditation and prayer, insisted on simplicity and austerity. Instead of a noblewoman, she wanted to be a hermit.

Had her father pushed back, had he tried to discipline her or quench her religious zeal, perhaps she would've had something to fight against and feed her fire. Instead, he told her, "You will rule this city one day, there's no escaping that. All you can choose is whether you want to be a good ruler or a bad one. That's entirely up to you."

She wanted to be a good ruler. But the idea of sitting under the silk canopy in the great hall of the palace seemed like a vague fantasy, a very distant future. Her father was only forty, he should have lived for decades more. She should have inherited Abia as a grown woman, mature and wise and versed in the art of ruling.

Not as an eighteen-year-old girl without a friend in the world.

Her father tried to teach her how to rule, but she has learnt too little. She knows nothing; she is just an overly serious, deeply shy girl who prefers silence and solitude. This city, the proud, rowdy, unapologetically beautiful Abia, doesn't need her.

Tears spill down Orsiana's cheeks, where the brisk wind dries them. She almost stands up, almost walks away. But the thought that she'd have to leave forever stops her. The city lies before her, basking in the sunshine. She spreads her arms, their curve following the curve of the city walls, and hugs Abia. She doesn't want to rule it, she wants to live with it and breathe with it and feel its heartbeat in her veins.

It makes all the difference in the world, little Orsiana, Veles told her, *whether you rule Abia or your uncle does.*

And perhaps she isn't very experienced or very wise, but she knows this: if Caril snatches Abia like a juicy low-hanging peach, he'll ruin it. He'll destroy the fine balance her father kept, he'll unleash his power-hungry friends, he'll let the Seragians in. He'll break the city's spine and bleed it dry, blind to everything but his own needs and desires.

She can't let him do it.

~

FEELING decisive and filled with purpose is good, but how is she going to beat Caril? Orsiana has no weapons and she doesn't want them, for there's been enough bloodshed. No, Caril thrives on confusion, on rumours and lies. Announcing that she's alive won't be enough, and after Veles' trick, she has no proof of it. She needs to beat Caril with deceit, not honesty.

Orsiana has been looking for allies in the wrong places.

She climbs down the harbour wall and walks back among the houses. There are no formal signs of mourning, no black flags in front of the palace, no public announcements, no town criers sharing the news. But by now, everybody knows Lord Orsolo is dead and his daughter is missing.

She needs to tell them what happened.

She looks for the sign she's seen many times walking down Booksellers' Alley, though she never needed those particular services: a large metal feather hanging from the post which juts out under a small first-floor window.

The bookbinder's shop smells of leather and glue, a familiar, comforting combination. Orsiana breathes in deeply as she closes the door behind her and asks, "Is the scribe upstairs?"

A boy carrying a bundle of green leather motions towards the back of the shop. "Yes, the stairs are over there."

She climbs the rickety staircase and knocks on the door.

"Come in," a voice says.

Orsiana steps into a room barely big enough for a large desk crammed by the window. A small, bald man puts down his quill. "Can I help you?"

"I need to write a letter," she says.

His quick, narrow eyes measure her up, and he immediately reaches for a cheap, thin sheet of paper. "Black ink or colour?" he asks. "If it's a love letter, may I suggest—"

"Good linen paper, please," Orsiana says, pulling a silver coin out of her pocket. "Black ink. And a quill, please. I'll write it myself."

"Excuse me? This is most—"

"Please. I'm in a hurry." She slides another silver besides the first. "Go and have a drink. By the time you return, I'll be done."

The scribe hesitates, wetting his dry lips with the tip of his tongue. Two silver crowns are enough to buy ten sheets of paper, a bottle of ink, and a flagon of wine. Orsiana knows it, but buying paper, quills, and ink, and then finding a quiet corner to write would take half a day. She doesn't have the luxury of time.

"All right," he gives in, placing a sheet of fine paper and a fresh quill before her. "Don't steal anything. I'll be downstairs, waiting for you to come out."

She dips the quill in ink and hesitates for a second. She doesn't know how to begin, there's no correspondence etiquette for such a letter.

The scribe turns at the door. "He's a lucky man." He winks at her and walks out.

Orsiana curses under her breath and starts writing. The words pour out, the recounting of the recent events, as clear and concise as possible. And yet, it's not a report. It's a friendly letter, a plea for help, a proposition. Also, it is a love letter of sorts, a young woman writing to a young man who once courted her, even if it was just a pleasant pastime with no real intention behind it. In the final paragraph, she quotes the young man's verses back at him:

"You once wrote, *If you walked with me in the evening among the fragrant roses, the moon would hide behind a cloud, shamed by the radiance of your face.* If those words were more than shiny beads of poetic imagination, help me now."

She signs the letter with her real name and seals it with hot wax. In the absence of her signet, she presses it with her thumb.

She runs downstairs, the letter safe in her pocket. The scribe is chatting with the boy and sipping wine from a wooden cup.

"I'm done," Orsiana says.

He throws her a quick glance, but as she's obviously not carrying bundles of paper or bottles of ink, he waves her away.

Now that she has her letter, she needs to find its recipient.

Orsiana grits her teeth as she enters The Olive Branch, steeling herself. The stories she heard from the clever young people her father gathered in the palace always described the wild, rowdy, noisy taverns where you could expect to be groped or hit with an empty mug at any time. But the interior of The Olive Branch is warm and well-lit, it smells of onions and beer, and people are too busy eating, drinking, and talking to pay any attention to one small dark-haired girl.

She musters the courage to walk to the barmaid. "I'm looking for Mareo," she says. "Have you seen him?"

The maid, a blonde twenty-something woman with arms so strong dockers would envy her measures Orsiana up. "Who wants to know?"

"I'm his cousin."

The maid raises an eyebrow, incredulous. "Sure you are. Don't try to sell your skinny rump here, wench, we have our own girls and boys."

Orsiana's cheeks flare up. "No, I really am his cousin. Mother sent me to check on Mareo because she heard there's been trouble at the palace, and if his patron is dead, he'll be out of work, won't he?" All that time she spent wandering around Abia with her father taught her the language of its streets. She emulates it now, its quick flow and its chopped final vowels, hoping it's convincing enough. "Look, I'm just here to make sure he's got somewhere to sleep and something to bite." She slips a coin into the maid's hand. "Can you tell me where he is?"

"Hasn't left his room since yesterday. Been moping about and drinking himself to stupor," the woman says. "Go up the stairs, the second door on the right. You may not like what you find."

Orsiana climbs to the first floor, rushes down the corridor and knocks. There is no answer, so she turns the knob. The door opens into a quiet room with shuttered windows. Its smell is a blend of familiar and unfamiliar—of books and ink and wine, and of a young, unwashed male burrowed in his musky lair.

"Mareo?" she calls softly.

The pile of bedding moves with a grunt and a handsome head with dark curls emerges from the mess. "Who are you?"

"Your cousin Bria, for the purposes of this conversation." She walks to the window and opens the shutters, letting in the golden afternoon light. "You need to get up."

"Leave me alone," the poet moans, pulling the sheet over his head.

She feels the urge to do just that, but a streak of stubbornness stops her. "Are you ill?"

"No," the heap of bed linen answers.

"Are you drunk?"

"No."

"Then what is wrong with you?"

He peers from under the sheet. "I am grieving, you nosy wench. You're no cousin of mine, they're all plump and ginger, with rabbit teeth. Now get lost."

She almost accuses him of being dramatic, but then the clear light reveals his bloated face and red-rimmed eyes. He's been crying.

His distress coaxes tenderness from her heart, but instead of crying with him, she asks, "What happened?"

"I lost my patron." He sniffs. "And I lost the loveliest girl in the world. My bright star, my inspiration—"

"Your star?"

"Gospa Orsiana."

Those words are an unexpected punch in the plexus, making her gasp.

He rubs the corners of his eyes and says, "She was in love with me."

"What?" Orsiana shakes her head, uncertain of her hearing. "Are you mad?"

He studies her, his gaze unkind, unimpressed. Orsiana swallows hard. She has imagined this encounter differently. Despite Veles' trick, she expected the young man who wrote her poems to recognize her somehow. That kind of connection was supposed to be transcendental. Yet all he can see is a plain girl in shabby clothes.

"But what would you know about love, you drab little goose?" He scratches his stubble. "Gospa Orsiana would let me stand so close to her I could feel her sweet breath on my skin. Once I brushed her breasts." He smirks. "Accidentally. She blushed prettily."

Orsiana feels like a character on stage, but she cannot decide whether it's a tragedy or a comedy. Somewhere deep underground, in his vast cavern, the snake god laughs.

"I have a job for you," she blurts out, eager to end his recollecting.

"Oh." His eyebrows shoot up. "I thought you were here to offer me your services."

Orsiana has known Mareo for two years, ever since he gained entrance to her father's circle, and he's always treated her with polite friendliness tinged with flirtation. It's quite a shock now to see him study and dismiss her as unimportant and unattractive. It tells her something about his true nature.

What was it that her father said? *Have your heart broken a little.* Yet this feels less like a romantic wound and more like a cold, sobering disappointment. If there ever was a girlish, soppy idea inside her head about a hero who would wrap his arms around her and kiss her and make everything right, it shrivelled and died in the hard light of Mareo's gaze.

Romance bloomed in the opulent chambers of the palace.

Here, in this tavern room, there's only transaction. Hence, she lets the insult slide like a raindrop from a leaf and pulls a gold coin out of her pocket. "I can pay."

His eyes glint at the sight of gold. After all, he did lose his patron and his position. "What do you need? A love poem for some clueless boy?"

"No." She takes a deep breath and steels herself, determined to keep her voice level. "I need a ballad about Lord Orsolo's murder. Ten stanzas, no more. You'll get another gold crown if you finish it before sunset."

"I don't ... why ..." He blinks and his brain catches up with his tongue. "Who sent you?"

"Someone important who wants the truth written down."

"And this truth, what is it?" He's still in bed, but now he's thinking, his tone cautious and calculated.

"It's all in here." She hands him the letter.

Colour drains out of his face as he reads it. He comes to the end and reads it again, then lifts his eyes to her. "Do you know what it says?"

"Yes, I've read it. Lord Caril and five members of the Great Council conspired to kill Gospodar Orsolo. They set a trap and murdered him in the garden of Caril's villa and spread the rumour that the Seragians did it. Caril's plan is to take Abia for himself. He also abducted Gospa Orsiana and tried to sell her to the slavers, but she escaped."

"Have you seen her? Is she unharmed?"

"She's alive and hiding in the city."

"I must help her." Mareo jumps out of his bed, stark naked, and Orsiana stares, unable to tear her eyes away. She's seen naked boys bathing in the summer, but never a grown-up man. The sight is less attractive than she thought. The poet pays no attention to her, but pulls his clothes on quickly. "Where is she? I want to see her."

"No, you mustn't know where she is, for your own safety," Orsiana says, her mouth dry. "And seeing you won't help her."

He splashes water on his face and runs wet fingers through his hair, trying to smooth it down. "She needs friends. I can take care of her."

It's almost sweet, this concern, despite his bragging about touching Orsiana. Perhaps Mareo does believe in heroic deeds and helping damsels in distress, but only if they're noble enough. Still, he misses the point completely.

"You can't take care of her," she says slowly. "This is a bloody coup. Therefore, she needs you to write a poem telling the truth. A murder ballad. Ten stanzas. This afternoon."

The icy tone of her voice stops his fretting. He scans the letter again. "Who else knows about this?"

"Nobody but the conspirators."

Mareo frowns, the impact of the dangerous secret written in broad strokes over his face. She doesn't hold it against him, quite the opposite. She's grateful he doesn't continue spewing big, fanciful words and empty threats. This is no time for bravado.

"I still don't understand why she sent you to me." He runs his fingers through his thick curls. "This is ..." He lowers his voice to a faint whisper. "Treason. Murder. She needs soldiers to fight for her, she needs the nobles to support her as the rightful heir, she needs the king to punish the traitors."

"Yes, she does, but she can't have them because they don't know what happened." Orsiana bites her lip. "Look, her uncle tried to sell her to Seragian slavers. She barely survived the escape. If she appears in Abia, Lord Caril will hunt her down before she gets the chance to tell what happened, and he'll make sure she disappears this time. She tried contacting powerful friends and it didn't go well. What she needs now is Abia on her side. The people need to know the truth."

"The truth?" He runs his fingers through his curls again. "And ... she needs me to write it down?"

"Orsiana told me you can weave magic with your words." A bit of flattery never hurt anyone. "She believes you're the best writer she knows. If anyone can take this," she points at the letter, "and turn it into something powerful, something that will move the citizens of Abia, it's you. They deserve to know what happened, and Orsiana deserves justice."

He lifts his eyebrows and there is a glimmer of challenge in his eyes. He's already putting the words together in his head. Looking for rhymes and metaphors, drumming the metre with his fingers. "She believes I'm the best?" he beams.

He is vain, and perhaps he has the right to be. His poetry is good, although Orsiana is now able to discern between the beautiful verses and the fickle, self-absorbed man who writes them. The dream of letting him steal a kiss or two lies abandoned in a heap of dirty linen on the floor.

"Of course, you can't sign this ballad if you want to keep your head attached to your neck," she says. "You do understand that, I presume?"

He looks stricken by the suggestion, but he nods.

"Look," she says, "if this plan goes right and Gospa Orsiana wins back what is rightfully hers, you'll be the most celebrated wordsmith in the history of this city. The one true hero. Just don't brag about it right now, for your own safety."

"Fine."

"I need it finished this afternoon," she adds.

Poetic indignation seeps out of his words as he says, "Poetry can't be rushed."

It's her turn to roll her eyes now. "Come on, you used to write funny jingles for tavern owners before Lord Orsolo took you in. You can write well and fast and precise."

He narrows his eyes. "You know, you sound just like—"

He doesn't say "Orsiana" aloud, but he's right, she sounds

just like the sharp, witty self he knew. The fact he can't recognize her now just because she wears a different face disappoints her.

"Write," she commands. "I'll go downstairs and fetch us some food."

"Don't forget the wine."

ORSIANA LEAVES Mareo's room with a poem in her pocket as the afternoon slowly melts into the evening, the colours of the sunset dyeing the sky pink and purple. Away from the harbour, the streets smell of cooking, people, and a hint of sewage. As the shadows lengthen, discomfort runs its cold fingers down her spine. What she plans to do is either a futile diversion or incendiary treason, and she can't predict which one it will turn out to be.

The city is not immune to a dose of self-mockery, and Kissing Alley has little to do with kissing. The houses on the both sides of the winding cul-de-sac are brothels, as respectable as these establishments go. There are no girls roaming outside, no drunken men chasing them. It's still early, the windows are open but no noise spills out, just some soft chatter and female laughter. The lamps are lit in the little alcoves beside the doors, though, signalling the houses are open for business.

Orsiana feels no contempt or disgust as she walks by. She's never entered a brothel, but she knows what happens in there. Her father insisted she learn about every corner of the city, regardless of its purpose. He abhorred ignorance. "Not knowing about something bad won't protect you from it," he claimed. "Quite the opposite."

The same principle was applied to the type of literature other fathers kept in locked cabinets in their chambers.

Orsiana was twelve when her father opened his library to her. "Read whatever you wish," he said. "If it disturbs you, come and we'll talk about it."

In theory, Orsiana is familiar with every nook and cranny of human character, with all its dark desires, moral failures, and depravity. This knowledge only arouses mild curiosity in her, though. She doesn't imagine herself as a creature ruled by passion.

In practice, she knows nothing, of course.

The house at the very end of Kissing Alley has no sign, no lamp in the alcove, nothing to signal it is anything but a private residence. Orsiana knocks on the door, waits, and knocks again. The door opens for a fraction, revealing the broad, bony face of a young woman. "Yes?"

"I need to speak with Mistress Divna on urgent business."

The owner's name makes the door open some more, letting out the harsh smell of printing ink. The young woman in an ink-stained apron still doesn't invite Orsiana in. "What business?"

"I need something printed discreetly."

Abia is a free town and the type of printing they do in Kissing Alley is not forbidden, but there are many who believe such things should never be published and are willing to impose their opinion by force.

The woman measures her up and decides Orsiana is no threat. "Come in," she says.

Orsiana steps into a narrow, whitewashed corridor, and from there, the young woman leads her into a comfortable office with a desk and two armchairs.

"Sit down, the Mistress will be with you shortly."

There is a bowl of sugared almonds on the desk. Orsiana grabs a handful and chews them quickly, too impatient to let the sugar melt on her tongue. She sat in that same office two months ago with her father, who was hunting for a rare edition of Forina's Love Poems with the most inspiring wood-cuts, and the memory of his amused chuckle when he opened it pierces her like a blade.

"I don't believe we've met," a woman says, entering the office. She's in her mid-thirties, tall, portly, with a thick red braid falling down her back. She wears a sensible grey dress and a leather apron.

"I need you to print something for me. Tonight," Orsiana says.

"Oh, and why should I do that?" The smile on Mistress Divna's face is not unfriendly, but her eyes are hard.

Coins won't persuade her, she has enough money. Therefore, Orsiana pulls the poem out of her pocket and hands it to the red-haired woman. "Just read it, please."

Mistress Divna takes it with a raised eyebrow, but as her eyes fly over the lines, her face blanches.

Mistaking her expression for confusion, Orsiana quickly adds, "I know it's not erotic poetry, but it's true, every word of it. The rumours that Gospodar Orsolo is dead fill every alley and tavern, but no one knows who did it, or how. It's important that the citizens of Abia learn what happened."

Unlike Mareo, the Mistress doesn't pelt Orsiana with questions. In fact, she ignores her completely, turning her face away, laying the poem gently on the table. Her jaw trembles while her neck and shoulders turn rigid, as if fighting against some immense force. A hard shiver rakes her body and a sob escapes her lips. She doubles over behind the desk, burying her face in her hands.

Orsiana sits quiet as a mouse, stunned by this display of grief. It's far too strong an emotion for someone who merely worked for her father, helping him find rare manuscripts and produce beautiful books, who was perhaps a friend, but nothing more—

Stupid, stupid Orsiana!

She remembers her father laughing softly in this very office, whispering something in Mistress Divna's ear. Their heads, pale gold and autumn red, bowed over a book. Mistress Divna pouring a drink for him, their fingers touching as she handed him the glass.

Intense discomfort makes Orsiana's skin crawl, the idea of her father and this woman, together, performing the ... acts ... so meticulously depicted in Mistress Divna's books.

The woman should be ashamed of herself for—

For what? Grieving for Orsiana's father? Sharing a bed with him?

Gospodar Orsolo never remarried after his wife's death. He rejected all offers from the noble families parading their pretty daughters before him, he escaped the claws of cunning widows and the sighs of blushing virgins, he never appeared in public with anyone but Orsiana beside him. He was discreet to a fault, so discreet that even Orsiana, sitting so many times in this very office with him, never suspected anything.

Did he do it to spare her feelings? Did he fear Orsiana would be judgemental and ungracious and selfish? A spoiled child who would deny her lonely, exhausted father a speck of warmth? She got so used to thinking of him as vulnerable and overwhelmed that she forgot he was a grown man, with needs and passions.

Orsiana's mortification, her burning cheeks, remain hidden from Mistress Divna only because the printer is still bent behind her desk. In the deepest, most private nook of her heart, Orsiana feels betrayed. Her father lied to her by omission; he had a whole secret life she knew nothing about.

She clears her throat, struggling with her feelings, grasping at politeness like a drowning sailor at wooden planks. "I am so sorry," she says, "I understand he was your friend."

The quiet sobs dwindle to shallow, jagged breathing. A hand grabs the edge of the desk and Mistress Divna emerges, revealing blotched, puffy skin and an unappealingly red nose. "A friend? Yes, I suppose you can call him that." Her fingers touch a small gold medallion nested between her collarbones. She doesn't bother to explain. Instead, she pulls a bottle of fig brandy and two ceramic cups from a drawer and pours one for herself and one for Orsiana.

"Let's drink to his lordship's memory," she says, raising her cup. "May the gods be as generous to him as he was generous to us."

Orsiana swallows her drink in one gulp, the fiery liquid burning her throat and setting at the bottom of her stomach like lava.

Raw emotion still lingers on Mistress Divna's face, but there's no apology, no shame. She takes in Orsiana's tattered clothes and tight-lipped embarrassment, her fingers wound like ivy around the cup. "And now, girl, tell me who sends you and what they want."

"I'm Lady Orsiana's maid," she says, her disguise feeling much thinner here than in Mareo's room. The poet had his head in the clouds and his heart in his crotch, he didn't see what was right before him. The printer is sharp as a shard of glass, despite the shock. It's almost as if she's playing along just to see the outcome. Orsiana swallows hard and continues, "My lady is alive and hiding in the city. She commissioned this ballad from a friend and needs you to print it, so that the citizens of Abia hear the truth about their lord's death."

Mistress Divna raises her eyebrows and a sad smile tugs at the corners of her mouth. "Are you ... Is your lady all right?"

Is she?

All Orsiana really wants to do is cry in somebody's arms until she has no more tears, but she can't afford to do that. So she bites the inside of her cheek instead, welcoming the immediate pain of wounded flesh.

Blood tastes like iron and earth in Orsiana's mouth. She manages to utter, "Will you help her?"

Mistress Divna inhales sharply and pauses before answering. "I'm not a coward and gods know I've happily printed dangerous things, but Lord Caril holds Abia now and he'll see this as treason. Does the lady understand that?"

"She does," Orsiana says with more confidence that she feels.

"And when the news spread, what is she going to do? Will she avenge her father's death? Will she fight for the city?"

"Fight?" Orsiana echoes, confused. "She'll expect the Council—"

"Look, this meeting makes me believe that you know her plans and have her ear," the Mistress says. "Gospa Orsiana needs to know that if she wants to do a man's job, she needs to be twice as cunning as any man. This is a great ballad." She taps the manuscript with her index finger. "It's that fiery pup, Mareo, isn't it? I'd recognize his rhymes anywhere."

"I don't—"

"Doesn't matter. What I want to say is—it's good. It will set the city on fire. And Caril will respond, with all his power, because his head will depend on it. So I'm asking you again, will the girl fight?"

It won't come to that, surely it won't. Orsiana doesn't want to spill more blood. She wants the citizens to force the Council to remove Caril, to lock him up for his crimes, and accept her as the true heir. Fighting is not a part of that plan.

That's not what the Mistress wants to hear, but Orsiana cannot lie to her.

"I don't know," Orsiana admits, wishing this was nothing more than a conversation between a scruffy maid and a publisher of obscene literature. Unimportant, informal.

Mistress Divna holds her gaze for a long time, and Orsiana feels the insecurity inside her burning like a beacon, rendering her skin translucent, colouring it a shameful hue of red. She doesn't dare look away, grinding her teeth so hard it makes her head hurt. At last, the Mistress gives her a curt nod.

"I'll print whatever she asks me to, but tell her this is the beginning, not the end. Is she wants Abia, she'll have to take it."

Orsiana wants to contradict her, argue, explain, but Mistress Divna gets up and marches out of the office with the poem in her hand. As soon as the door closes behind her, Orsiana takes a deep, ragged breath. What is she doing?

May the gods help her.

~

IT IS ALMOST midnight when the printing is done. The apprentice opens the office door and carries in two large bundles. The noise wakes Orsiana, dozing in the chair, her body curved into a tight ball.

The girl sets the poems on the desk and nods to Orsiana. "Two thousand copies," she says. "The Mistress wishes you good luck."

Orsiana stifles a yawn. "Thank you."

The apprentice clearly wants her out, but Orsiana takes a moment to appreciate Mistress Divna's skill. Even though the paper is cheap, the letters are black and crisp, the title—The Murder of Gospodar Orsolo—catching the eye immediately. There is even a picture of a bleeding dagger underneath it, which is tawdry but effective. Mareo would approve.

"It's beautiful," Orsiana says. "Please tell the Mistress that we're grateful—"

"Yes, yes." The apprentice urges her to get out. "Just make sure the bastard pays for his crimes." And then she shuts the door firmly behind her.

Orsiana hauls the leaflets down Kissing Alley, where the

atmosphere is more lively now, and pauses at the corner of the next street. Summer nights are short; she has less than five hours left until dawn. She needs to go to private houses and push the poem under their doors, and to taverns; leave it folded on the tables when no one is watching. No villas, no noble houses. Merchants are fine, and so are craftsmen and artists. Fishermen and labourers usually can't read, so she doesn't need to go down there, they'll hear about it in the morning.

Abia is a big town, but its houses are crammed together, and Orsiana distributes the last sheets before the first light of dawn appears in the east. She is bone tired and her feet hurt, but her heart is aflame. She knocks on the back window of a bakery and buys a fresh bun, so hot she can barely hold it. Then she finds a cheap, austere inn, pays for a pallet in the common room and throws herself on it, asleep as soon as her head touches the pillow.

~

IN THE MORNING, Abia buzzes like an angry beehive.

Orsiana leaves the inn and before she turns the first corner, she already sees a man reading Mareo's poem to his three companions. With her heart pumping fiery hope through her veins, she walks towards the port. On every street corner, there is at least one person reading the poem aloud, a handful of people gathered around them. "The Death of Gospodar Orsolo" is recited by hundreds of mouths, heard by thousands of ears.

She comes closer to a young lawyer sitting on a window sill above the crowd, reading with a deep, resonant voice, and marvels at how Mareo's words flow like a silver stream when spoken, enchanting the audience even when describing a horrible murder. Their beauty feels like a tribute to all the beauty her father collected in his lifetime, an epitaph for a man who spent a fortune supporting artists. And yet, the poem is not an elegy, but a catchy, rhythmical ballad that slips into your ears and brain, calling for justice and revenge.

The men in the crowd thumb the handles of their knives and daggers, ball their fists and exchange dark looks, mouthing the words, tasting them on their tongues, and then disperse, the fire of truth already lit in their hearts.

In the afternoon, the mood in the streets turns hotter, more intense. There are no more poems in plain sight because Caril's guards are now roaming Abia, confiscating every sheet they can get their hands on, but it's all that people talk about.

"The Great Council should have this investigated," they whisper.

And, "The king should know about this."

Orsiana holds her tongue and listens to the grumbling of the town distilling its grief to anger. Confusion and doubt still dilute the rage, but they will soon evaporate in its heat. A moment of doubt grabs her when she hears a young man talking about storming the palace. Has she woken a monster? There's no way to put it back to sleep now, she can only jump on its back and ride it. Mistress Divna warned her she would have to fight for Abia, but the fight Orsiana wants involves words, and law, and justice, not blades and blood.

When it gets dark, Orsiana passes by a crowded tavern and hears Mareo's words already set to music. A young woman is singing them, accompanied by a harp, and people listen in silence, the usual rowdiness muted for once. When two men in Caril's livery try to interrupt her, shouting insults, a group of men throw them out unceremoniously and return to the tavern to listen to the singer.

At midnight, she sees Mareo reciting his own words at The Olive Branch, packed to the rafters.

"Are you mad?" she hisses when he jumps off the table,

followed by cheers and calls for more. "It's supposed to be anonymous."

"They don't know I wrote it," he retorts, beaming, while a barmaid hands him a cup of strong red wine. "I just enjoy saying it out loud."

Orsiana has spent enough time with artists to understand this pride in one's work—after all, she hired him precisely because his poems are good—but there is a part of her that abhors turning her personal tragedy into a spectacle. The poem is poignant, but the crowd hangs on the gory details, on the explicit violence. It's the blood they want, not the solemn mourning.

It's a trick, she reminds herself, a trap for Caril to fall in. Mourning in silence would just empower him. If she wins, there will be plenty of time to properly honour her father's legacy.

"Just be careful," she warns Mareo. "Not all people who cheer you are your friends. And many lesser poets are surely jealous of your talent and know your style. If just one of them betrays you to Gospodar Caril, you'll be in trouble."

"Don't be silly," he scoffs. "Abia loves her poets and the lord has bigger troubles now than hunting me down."

She shakes her head in disagreement, but before she can say anything else, the crowd pulls him back on the table and the performance starts anew.

Caril will be worried in the palace, but not panicked. He still has the councillors on his side, and his guards, and plenty of money. He's never cared much about public opinion and it's unlikely that the anger on the streets will smoke him out. But Orsiana counts on the other councillors and nobles, who had nothing to do with the coup, to listen to the streets and grow worried and demand answers. They are the lever she hopes to move.

It's almost midnight when she returns to the cheap inn,

lies on her thin pallet and dreams of sea maidens and snakes while other women snore around her.

Shouts wake her before dawn and she opens her eyes to see the orange glow of fire reflected off the night mist. She runs out of the inn and down towards the harbour. Caril's warehouse is burning. Dozens of people form a chain, handing buckets of seawater, fighting to put out the flames. If the fire spreads, it will swallow the surrounding warehouses, or even spread to the ships. Luckily, the night air is humid, there is no wind, and the blaze is soon contained, but the warehouse is lost. It burns down to blackened beams, grey ash, and charred, soggy remains of fine goods. The air reeks of burnt cinnamon and cloves.

At first light, just as the tired firefighters retreat, Caril sweeps in with his retinue and the sight of his face distorted in anger sends a little shudder of satisfaction down Orsiana's spine. War has been declared.

In the morning, there's more men in Caril's livery on the streets, and not only do they confiscate and destroy every copy of the poem they find, they also question and harass everyone found with it. The citizens push back, though, and fights flare up all across Abia.

Orsiana walks around the town, but this time she's not interested in taverns and crowds—she knows their opinion already. She sneaks into merchant's warehouses, ship owner's offices, and expensive shops and registers the mood there. The atmosphere brims with caution and fear. Although a man of business himself, Caril has made it clear that he thinks the lucrative contracts should go to patrician families, and that commoners should not get richer than the lords. In the days since Lord Orsolo's death, Caril has done nothing to retract that claim. The merchants of Abia—a vast majority of them commoners by birth—wait for his next move with suspicion and hostility.

Then she stops by the noble houses, which are still silent, trying to figure out how much they stand to gain with Caril's ascension. They didn't like Orsiana's father, and Caril has so far declared he's on their side. They'll turn against him only if it becomes obvious that he cannot keep the city in his grasp.

Orsiana fears that, like any other novelty, the excitement the poem roused will soon die down. She has seen her father quench more serious public discontent by talking with the citizens' representatives and bringing their issues up before the Council.

But Caril misjudges the situation; underestimates the anger brewing inside the city walls. He does nothing to explain his brother's death, no Seragian assassins are brought to justice, his witnesses refuse to show their faces in public. Lord Orsolo's body is not placed on view to allow the citizens to pay their respects, and there is no talk of the funeral ceremony. Orsiana's destiny remains a mystery and wild rumours that she is planning to take back what is hers start to circulate the taverns.

"Why isn't the Council discussing succession?" Orsiana whispers into Mareo's ear that night at The Olive Branch and he shouts it to his enthralled audience after one of his fiery performances of the ballad. The crowd responds with a roar and the question spreads like wildfire. The next morning, even the boy who sells clams on the docks is asking it, musing about the rulers of Abia as if he attended weekly briefings in the palace.

The cat and mouse game lasts for eight days. Each day, Caril gets more nervous and his guards more brutal. He loses the support of the palace guard—the captain of the guard leaves and almost all his men leave with him. Caril replaces the guards with mercenaries; they descend upon Abia like wolves and the citizens respond with violence.

Trade grinds to a halt. Shops close, merchants hire their

own mercenaries to guard their warehouses and mansions, foreign ships flee the port, patricians retreat to their hunting lodges and country estates. The poor build barricades in the streets and sharpen their blades.

Caril is forced to call the Great Council, but the councillors refuse to enter the palace and risk being trapped in the great hall. Instead they insist they meet in the open, like their ancestors, in the town loggia, and Caril has no choice but to appear there.

Orsiana watches the meeting from the crowd. Her uncle, who's never walked among the citizens of Abia as their equal or attempted to feel the pulse of the city, appears decked out in ceremonial velvet and fur, despite the heat, and demands the councillors to confirm he's the rightful ruler of Abia. Behind the cordon of mercenaries, the people watch the Council in ominous silence, so atypical for the rowdy crowd that it sends a shiver down Orsiana's spine.

"Where is Gospa Orsiana?" a councillor asks. "Before we know what happened to her, we cannot decide on the succession."

Orsiana supposes Caril would love to say she is dead and settle the question once and for all, but even a man as tone-deaf as him understands the crowd will tear him apart if he says that.

"All I know is that she disappeared after the attack," he says at last, and faces a hail of whistles and jeers. He tries to quieten them with a wave of his hand, and when he doesn't succeed, he raises his voice. "But if she's here in Abia, I'm calling her to show herself. She has nothing to fear. As her uncle, I will help her choose what is best for her."

The hissing and booing stops only when the gaunt, ancient Councillor Zentio steps forward, holding a letter. He is known for his sharp tongue that always gets straight to the point, and no one is surprised when he sets upon Caril. "I have news for you, you obtuse, incompetent fool. The king is coming to deal with this mess you caused. Step down and tell us what happened to the rightful heiress before he arrives."

Caril doesn't budge. "Do we fear the king now?" he retorts, his face crimson. "Shall we let him tell us how to rule our city? No, I'll shut the gates and let him sit outside until I decide what to do." He turns away from the councillors and faces the crowd. "No stranger is going to tell us what to do. Not the king, and certainly not the lying coward who wrote that deceitful dirge about my brother's death. There are still laws and customs in this city."

"Do you deny its truth?" Councillor Vaneo, a merchant, shouts. "Where are those Seragian assassins you promised to arrest? Where are the witnesses? Where is your niece?"

Caril flashes his teeth in rage, but before he can answer, someone from the crowd shouts, "Murderer!" and raises a roar of fury from the citizens. The Council splits into two opposing parties, and the whole meeting dissolves into chaos. The guards barely manage to drag the frothing councillors away from the deadly mob, and Orsiana escapes to a side alley, squashed, bruised, and terrified.

She wanted the Great Council to turn against Caril, to dismantle his hold over the city and force him to retreat, but the king is bad news for Abia. Although the town and its surrounding province of Larion have been a part of the Amrian Kingdom for three hundred years—ever since they opened their doors and bent their knees before Amris the Golden-Haired—no king has ever interfered in the affairs of the city. To do so now would be a terrible abuse of the royal power.

And yet, no king can allow a city as important as Abia to sink into bloody anarchy. Especially not a young king, like Amron V, who has only recently inherited the throne and still has to establish his authority. If he wants other lords in his kingdom to obey, he will have to restrain Caril. And the citizens of Abia will see it as an attack on their independence, no matter how much they might hate Orsiana's uncle.

Orsiana's time is running out. And so is her luck.

~

WHEN SHE ARRIVES at The Olive Branch at sunset on the ninth day, the blonde barmaid greets her. "Your cousin needs you upstairs," she says, looking pale and worried. Her demeanour doesn't alarm Orsiana; everybody looks pale and worried in Abia. She rushes upstairs and barges into the poet's room.

"What do you—"

Mareo lies on the floor, bruised and bloody, his hands tied, his mouth gagged, and moans in panic at the sight of her.

The door slams behind Orsiana. As she spins around, a fist collides with her jaw. The world explodes in pain; she falls down. The shock paralyzes her: she cannot move, she cannot speak. A man picks her up and hoists her over his shoulder like a sack of wheat.

The pain fogs her mind; her thoughts fly away like frightened sparrows. The man carries her down the darkening streets, blood dribbling from the corner of her mouth and leaving a trail on the cobbles.

The palace looks unfamiliar when he carries her in, every angle distorted, every upside-down shape wrong. They descend into the shadows, into a badly lit cell, among the faces she has never seen. Someone ties her to a chair, someone pours a bucket of water over her head.

Somewhere near, Mareo screams. "I don't know, I don't know."

Orsiana sobs hearing his agony, and tugs at the rope in vain. Too distraught to pray properly, she sends a desperate plea to any god who may hear her, *Spare him, please, he did this because he cares about me. Don't punish him for love.* But the cell walls are so thick not even thoughts can escape them.

Mareo betrays her in the end, of course, tells the whole story of the girl who commissioned a poem from him, but there's no useful information in his words, nothing about Orsiana, no conspiracy, nothing. He screams and sobs and pleads, and then he stops. The silence is worse than the noise.

Orsiana knows it's her turn when Caril walks in, a shadow among the shadows. "Where is Orsiana?" he asks.

"Here," she says.

A man grabs her hand, pulls her finger backwards until it breaks.

"Where is Orsiana?" Caril repeats. Orsiana's fingers snap like twigs and she screams and begs and tells them stories that sound like fever dreams, about sea maidens and snake gods. They don't believe a word she says, they think she's mocking them, so they hurt her until she can speak no more.

"She's useless," Caril says at last.

A cord bites into the soft skin of her neck and cuts off the light.

3

THE MIRACLE OF LOVE

rsiana opens her eyes. Everything around her is bright green, with gem-like specks of yellow, red, and blue. She lies on a silken carpet of grass strewn with wildflowers, under the warm caress of the summer sunlight. The air is fragrant and still, the silence broken only by the buzzing of the bees. She breaths in deeply and immediately moans in pain. Every movement of her chest sends a wave of agony through her body. Her throat feels raw, her cheekbones bruised, her teeth loose in a cracked jaw. Her fingers refuse to move, black and swollen.

"Oh, you poor little sparrow. Does it hurt much?"

Orsiana groans in response. A pair of delicate bare feet approach her, trailing a gauzy white gown, and when she looks up, she sees a young woman of impossible beauty smiling at her.

"Oh, what have they done to you, disfigured you so," the woman says. "And Veles, that beast ..." Gentle hands touch Orsiana's face. "Come, I'll help you get up."

"I don't think I can walk," Orsiana rasps. She cannot feel her legs.

"It's just a few steps, come." The woman wraps her arms around Orsiana's torso, hoists her up.

Orsiana screams in pain. Her injured legs refuse to support her and she falls into the woman's arms like a rag doll. The woman is only slightly larger than Orsiana; the impact should throw her off balance, yet she doesn't budge.

"All right, I'll carry you then," she says, and lifts Orsiana without any sign of effort.

Broken bones grind against each other inside Orsiana and she screams again. "Put me down, please, put me down."

"We're already here," the woman says.

From the corner of her eye, Orsiana sees a little pool, crystal blue and still as a mirror. She's very thirsty, but she doesn't understand why the pool is so important when every part of her body is burning in pain.

The woman kneels down, still holding Orsiana. "I'll lower you into the pool now," she says. "Don't worry, it's shallow."

"No, why—"

The water is warm, and as soon as it touches her injured limbs, the pain abates.

"Hold your breath, now," the woman says. She puts her hand on top of Orsiana's head and pushes down. Orsiana sinks and closes her eyes. The water supports her, makes her weightless, while the pain ebbs away, leaving only gentle tingling.

She surfaces, taking large gulps of air, marvelling at her lungs expanding without pain, at her legs moving at her command, at her face feeling whole and smooth again.

"That's better." The woman smiles and Orsiana notices her eyes are not cornflower blue, as she thought, but black with a golden swirl of stars inside them.

"Oh," Orsiana says, "you must be—"

"Lada." The Goddess of Love smiles and Orsiana, who's never been attracted to girls, feels a sudden urge to kiss her.

She clears her throat, banishing the impulse, and motions at the glittering water around her. "And this is your fountain of youth."

"Drink," the Goddess commands. "It feels good, doesn't it?"

Orsiana drinks and it does feel good. It feels like a burden she didn't know she was carrying is finally lifted. Careful not to make ripples, she studies her reflection in the pool, wondering what magic it worked on her besides the healing. It isn't youth, obviously; if she were any younger, she'd be a child. But there's something strange about …

Then it strikes her. She's herself again; the disguise Veles gave her has been washed away. Her face is her own again, although … it's slightly more symmetrical now, with darker lashes and eyebrows. Her skin, always clear and smooth, glows from the inside, translucent like alabaster. And her soft, unruly hair has become a thick, silken mass of gentle waves.

"But I don't want—" she starts and loses courage before Lada's eerie eyes. "I'm afraid that people will see me now, and I don't want to be seen."

The Goddess smiles and Orsiana remembers that love is not always kind. "It is your destiny to be seen, little Orsiana. People will raise their eyes to your golden light, and they will look up to you, for wisdom, and guidance, and strength."

The words ring like a prophecy, and not a cheerful one.

"But that's not the life I want." Orsiana wants peace, silence, private moments with the people she cares about.

"Well, that's the life you get." Lada's smile is brilliant and cold, like a ray of sunshine reflecting off a frozen lake. "You have a clear purpose, which is more than most people could say."

The burden of duty descends upon Orsiana's shoulders once more like a heavy cloak.

"And one more thing," the Goddess says. "You're lovely now, but I need you to be enchanting."

"What? Why?"

"Because there's a great love coming your way. A union that will change the history of the kingdom."

Orsiana is sick of history, bone-tired of divine purpose and terrified of the Gods' scheming. She feels goaded, pushed around like a figure on the game board. Why did Korab save her from drowning, why did Veles hide her from Caril's murderous claws? And why is Lada patching her up now, sending her back into the fight without telling her the real reason they've all set their divine eyes upon her? It's not for Orsiana that they're doing this, she realizes. She is just a tool.

"No, please," she begs.

"You'll thank me later." Lada's hand cups the back of Orsiana's head, drawing her close. Orsiana gasps, but no mortal can resist the kiss of the Goddess of Love. Their lips meet and pleasure surges through Orsiana's body, hot and irresistible. Ravenous for more, she closes her eyes and leans deeper into the immortal embrace.

QUICK, light fingers touch Orsiana's body and she opens her eyes to see a scruffy boy searching through her clothes. "Back off," she barks and the boy yelps in surprise.

"I thought you were dead," he says.

"I'm not." She sits up on the hard ground and looks around. The boy kneels beside her, a stone wall behind him. Further in the distance the tall, gaunt silhouettes of cypresses reach towards the sky. She touches the rough sackcloth entangled around her legs. Half a dozen other sacks lie on the ground beside her. No, not sacks. Her nose recognizes the unmistakable odour of death.

"What is this place?" she asks the boy.

"The cemetery," he says.

"How did I get here?"

"They bring the dead from the palace every night and bury them in the common grave." He tugs at the next sack, turns over the body. Moonlight falls on Mareo's face.

In a flash, everything comes back to Orsiana: the dungeons, the questioning, the torture. The pain still reverberates in her bones. She crawls to Mareo, pushes the boy away, and lays her cheek against the poet's. Her lips brush his dry, ice-cold mouth in a senseless attempt to breathe some life into him. Shaking him she pleads, "Wake up, please." She cups his bristly cheeks, willing him to open his eyes. "Come on."

The touch of divine that clings to her heels does not extend to others, though.

"He's dead as a doornail, can't you see?" the boy says.

"Leave me alone, you filthy vulture!"

He shrugs and starts searching the next body in the row, while she cradles Mareo in her arms. He looked perfectly weightless when he recited his poetry, filled with nothing but fiery breath, but now his body lies heavy like a lump of cold, damp clay, and she knows he is truly dead.

The boy comes back, touches her shoulder.

"Look, I'm glad you're alive, but the guards will be back soon, and if they find you here, they'll finish the job." He motions at Mareo. "Are you so eager to join your sweetheart?"

Orsiana doesn't know whether to curse the little robber or thank him, so she shakes her head and kisses Mareo's cheek, bidding him farewell. Then she scurries away, slipping behind the black cypresses. Her body works perfectly, unbroken, lithe. Memories of blood and agony tug at her brain, but she pushes them away. Not now.

The graves lie silent in the moonlight as she sneaks among them, feeling the gravel under the thin soles of her sandals, touching the rough headstones. She wanders the winding paths for a while, still stunned by the sight of the sacks lined up for a hasty burial. Caril is killing people and he won't stop until he finds her; the longer she hides, the more people will get hurt. Mistress Divna was right: if Orsiana wants Abia, she'll have to fight for it.

She shuts her eyes as a wave of anguish washes over her. How is she supposed to fight if she has no money, no power, no allies left in this city? The moment she steps on the streets of Abia, she will be recognized. If Caril catches her first, he'll kill her. If someone else catches her, then the Council might ...

"Oh, damn the Council!" she whispers. A bunch of quarrelsome old men—they won't do anything, they're too afraid of Caril. They'll bicker and threaten, but they won't rise up in arms. And if what Councillor Zentio said is true, and the king is on his way, it will make matters infinitely worse. Caril is ready to shut the gates of Abia. If the king tries to force his way in, there will be a bloodbath. If he doesn't, Caril will become a hero, the man who bent the king to his will. There is no happy outcome. Unless ...

Unless Orsiana gets to the king before he reaches Abia.

Withdrawing as far from the sacks filled with murdered people as her legs will carry her, she strays among the tombs of the distinguished citizens, of those with enough power and money to make their final resting places imposing. All those mausoleums look the same to her now, bathed in the weak, silvery moonlight. They loom like strange, excessively adorned little mansions of death, complete with their lifelike statues, watching Orsiana with their empty eyes.

She wonders what happened to her father's body. There was no public burial, no ceremony, no mention of his remains. The thought opens a chasm of grief in her heart, but she pushes it down into the darkness, with other things she must avoid if she wants to go on. Her father would have wanted her to remember him alive, as he was when they roamed the streets of Abia together.

Or when they roamed the gravelled paths of this cemetery together.

Orsiana stops in her tracks as the ghostly fingers of midnight fog touch the back of her neck. There's something important here, something she must remember.

From the murky bottom of her childhood memories, a day at the cemetery emerges, a sunny spring afternoon. She couldn't have been older than ten, because both her brothers were still alive, and her father still visited the family crypt to talk to his late wife. She held his hand as they climbed the gentle slope and he named the ancient families.

"See how they have a ship carved above the entrance? They started as captains and got very rich," he said. "And then your great-grandmother's family, the Farians, they have an hourglass and a skull. They were all rather morbid." He pushed the wrought iron gate and beckoned Orsiana to follow him. "There's something I need to show you."

They entered into the dim, dry interior, where marble slabs hid the caskets of her ancestors. The thought of the bodies stacked there didn't scare her; she was comfortable around the dead. Her mother was dead, after all, her image a bas-relief profile in white marble, surrounded by flowers. When Orsiana talked to her sometimes, she felt warmth on her face, like sunlight kissing her skin. Here, however, in the tomb of her great-grandmother's family, there was only cool silence. These dead didn't recognize her or care for her presence.

"See this trapdoor?" her father asked, pointing at the heavy iron lid on the floor. "When Seragians first threatened to invade Larion, the Farian family built an underground tunnel here. My grandmother showed it to me when I was a boy."

She was intrigued, imagining spies, chases, and trysts. "Can we go in and explore?"

"Gods, no." Her father shuddered. "Tunnels give me severe claustrophobia. But if you ever need to leave the city without anyone seeing you, this is the way. Promise me you won't use it to elope with some kitchen boy."

She smiled. "What if he's a prince in disguise?"

"Especially not if he's a prince in disguise." He shook his head in faint rebuke. "And don't tell anyone about it. This is a family secret."

"A family secret." The sunlit vision of her father fades, but the memory remains. A hourglass and a skull, that's what she's looking for. She walks with a purpose now, certain that she remembers the position of the mausoleum: turn right around the corner, behind those cypresses. If she finds it, she will be able to sneak out of Abia without anyone noticing.

"Who goes there?" Two guards materialize on the path to her left.

Orsiana freezes, hoping to blend into the leafy background, but a treacherous ray of moonlight illuminates her arm, making her skin shine like alabaster.

"Must be one of those cursed little thieves," one of the guards mutters. "Come here! If you show us where your friends are, we won't beat you."

There's no point in negotiating or playing stupid. Without a word, Orsiana dashes in what she hopes is the right direction.

"Hey! Stop!" They run after her, their booted feet faster on the gravel than her flimsy sandals.

Memory or sheer luck lead her to the right mausoleum. The wrought iron door is unlocked. She pushes it and ducks behind it, her heart drumming wildly. There are more voices outside now, shouting. "Search the mausoleums in this row," someone orders. "You start from this side, and you from the other one."

Orsiana turns in the almost complete darkness and steps

forward. Her feet move from the marble slabs to cold iron. A trapdoor, she remembers. Kneeling down, she feels for the handle and finds a padlock. She pulls at it, but it doesn't budge, despite the flakes of rust peeling under her fingers.

"This one is clear." She hears the guards outside. "This one too." They're coming nearer.

She has nowhere to hide. If they catch her, someone is bound to recognize her, and then she's dead.

She must break the padlock. She feels around blindly. No crowbars, no useful tools, nothing. But her fingers find a heavy marble vase which is not attached to the wall. She can barely lift it, but if she hits the rusty padlock with it …

The iron clangs like a bronze bell, filling the small chamber with sound.

"Over here!" someone shouts outside.

Orsiana hits the padlock again and again, growling with effort, until it breaks. Just as she grabs the handle and pulls the trapdoor, torchlight pours through the gate.

"Stop right there!"

The trapdoor swings open and without looking down, Orsiana jumps.

She falls down a narrow shaft and hits the ground hard. Her ankles and knees absorb the shock unwillingly, sending a wave of pain up her body. A moment later, she's crawling through a narrow tunnel. The darkness is complete, but she can hear the guards shuffling above. She must go on or get caught like a dirty sewer rat.

She moves on all fours, light and nimble, her size finally an advantage. She cannot see where she's going, but the tunnel leads straight ahead and she can only hope it's not blocked or flooded. Feet hit the ground behind her and somebody shouts, "Give me that torch, it's pitch black," but by the time they get their light, she's already out of reach, a quiet ghost scurrying through the narrow passage.

It can't be longer than three hundred paces, yet it seems like an eternity. The air is stale and so bad it makes her dizzy, but she crawls, following the tunnel on its gentle slope downwards and then up again. The men fall behind, cursing and making a terrible noise as they struggle to get through, but they don't give up.

The tunnel ends in a wooden trapdoor low enough for her to reach. She pushes it open and grabs the frame. Fear fills her muscles with unexpected strength and she pulls her body up. She's in an olive grove just outside the city, the trapdoor hidden in a ring of ancient trees. She slams the trapdoor shut. There are stones around her that she could pile on top of it, but she doesn't know how far behind the soldiers are and she doesn't want to guess.

Orsiana turns and runs across the uneven, stony terrain. She barely makes a dozen paces when the trapdoor opens. "There she is!" someone shouts and the chase begins anew, up the terraced hill divided by dry stone walls. Her pursuers are so close she can hear their panting and any moment now she expects their hands on her body or their steel cutting into her flesh.

Like enchanted forest creatures, three shadows step out from behind the olive trees. Orsiana screams and stumbles. One shadow catches her while the other two attack the men chasing her. She struggles, but the shadow turns out to be compact and strong and entirely human.

"We're the king's guard, don't be afraid," he whispers. "Wait here." Then he jumps into the skirmish, slashing with his sword.

It's all over before she has the time to catch her breath and calm her thundering heart. Orsiana's pursuers surrender, and the attackers take their weapons and tie their hands.

"Take them to the camp, we'll question them later," says the man who caught Orsiana. The moonlight reveals that he's tall and young, but his face remains blurry and all Orsiana can see is the flash of his teeth when he smiles at her. "Secret passage?" he asks.

"What?"

"You appeared out of nowhere and you clearly came from Abia. So, the passage. Where is it?"

Orsiana bites her lip, considering her options. If the soldiers search the area carefully, certain that there must be a passage somewhere, they will find the trapdoor. Still, she asks, "Why do you need it?"

The man offers her his hand and pulls her up. A mixture of leather, horse, and sweat hits her nostrils. The top of her head barely reaches his shoulder.

"It would be awfully convenient if we could sneak into Abia and take the palace before dawn. This whole shitstorm would be over by tomorrow."

"When you say 'we', you mean ..."

"The king's men, the vanguard. We've just arrived, the rear is still up there on the road. I bet that bastard in the palace doesn't know we're here yet. By the time the sun rises, it'll be obvious, and we'll lose any advantage we have now. We'll sit here like ducks and negotiate and bargain and lay siege if we have to. But if we get into Abia tonight ..." He opens his hands and motions towards the city, challenging her to see how perfectly simple it would all be.

"And the king, has he arrived?" she asks.

"Not yet. I want to surprise him, I want to open the gates of Abia for him." He smiles again. "I'm Liran, the captain of his guard."

"Bria." Her maid's name slips smoothly off her tongue.

"Well, Bria, what are you doing here?"

"Running away from Abia." She looks at the dark outline of the city walls behind her and then at the young captain who saved her, and makes a decision. "And running back in, obviously."

~

LIRAN GATHERS his men so quickly Orsiana has no time to question her decision. No enemy, no foreign army has entered Abia since Amris conquered it and established the kingdom more than three hundred years ago. But the king is not an enemy of Abia, she tells herself. It's Caril, a worm burrowed deep in the apple, poisoning it from the inside.

"Can I talk to you?" she whispers to Liran as his men wait for his command.

The young captain looks impatient, ready for a fight, but still he steps aside. "What is it?"

Among the olive trees, the soldiers wait. They use no light and keep their silence with such discipline that she feels both admiration and dread.

"I need you to promise me there will be no bloodshed," she says. "Abia shouldn't pay for Caril's crimes, and I won't betray it to the king's guard just to see it bleed."

"We're doing this to avoid bloodshed." He's restless, aching for action, every inch of him brimming with energy. Orsiana has little experience with soldiers, they make her uneasy, and she reminds herself she should be cautious. And yet, there is something direct, no-nonsense about this man that makes her trust him.

"All right," she concedes. "I'll show you how to enter." She retraces her footsteps over the stony ground, leading two dozen men to the ring of ancient olive trees and the trapdoor hidden in its midst.

At the cemetery, as his men pour out of the dark crypt, Liran says, "You've done me a great favour. When we remove the usurper from the palace, come find me and you'll be rewarded."

His words are a slap.

"No," she says. "I'm not doing it for a reward. I'm doing it because Caril is going to destroy this town."

There's no time for discussion, and yet he doesn't ignore her or simply push her aside. Surprise rings in his voice when he asks, "Who are you?"

"Someone who's been injured by the recent turn of events. I need you to take me with you."

He looks her over, though there's not much to see in the dark. "I don't think that a girl should—"

"Do you want me to show you around the palace or not?" she snaps. "I grew up in it, I know every nook and cranny. Without me, Caril will vanish before you catch him."

"Fine." He turns away from her, groups his men and leads them to the Northern Gate. The guards suspect nothing and they are disarmed and tied up before they get the chance to raise an alarm. Liran's men open the city gate and the king's troops pour in.

She leads them through the dark residential streets, where the fear of the recent skirmishes has closed the shutters and barred the doors. If anyone sees them, they don't make a sound. Too many high-strung, sharp-bladed mercenaries have been prowling the streets lately for the citizens to dare complain about their presence. The restless city sleeps heavily in the pre-dawn hours.

They approach the palace from the rear, avoiding the vast white expanse of the square. The great building was designed for beauty, not defence: its walls are porous, letting through anyone who knows their way. Orsiana leads them to a small back entrance, unguarded, secured by a flimsy lock, and from it to the quarters of the palace guard.

"Please don't kill anyone if you can help it," she repeats her plea. "There's been enough bloodshed already."

The mercenaries put up a fight, while Liran moves on with a group of men and follows Orsiana upstairs. The first floor is mostly offices. The palace never sleeps, though, and a few red-eyed clerks poke their heads around the doors. Some retreat immediately, leaving the fighting to those who are paid for it. Some look as if they're ready to shout, but when Orsiana hisses, "Back to work," they stare at her wide-eyed, as if they've seen a ghost, and retreat without a word.

Up on the second floor, the guards are prepared for their coming, warned by the sounds of struggle. They block the entrance to the lord's chambers in a futile attempt to stop Liran and his men. It doesn't even slow them down: they break in like the tide, crashing through the doors, rolling over everyone who stands in their way.

Orsiana has a hunch where to find her uncle, and she is not wrong: Caril slithered into Lord Orsolo's study, a treacherous snake pretending to be the rightful ruler. When Liran storms in with half a dozen men, swords in their hands, Orsiana trails quietly behind them.

Despite the soldiers stinking of sweat, metal, and dirt, the familiar scent hits Orsiana's nostrils as soon as she walks in: dust and leather, wine and beeswax, and a hint of her father's personal scent, vetiver and lemon, as if he's just walked across the room, trailing it behind him. Candlelight reveals the usual mess: the cluttered desk, the cabinets filled with curiosities, the strange instruments balanced precariously on narrow shelves, like giant insects. The study feels like a refuge from the horrors of the night, as if her father's spirit still protected it.

Yet, instead of her father, Caril stands beside the desk in his elegant black silk, self-assured and unrepentant, staring coldly at the intruders. If he's afraid, he doesn't show it. "How dare you barge into the palace like this? Who sends you?"

"We are the king's guard," Liran says.

Caril remains unimpressed. "No messenger, no uniforms, just blades in the dark. How very ... Amrian. If the king wants to speak to me, he can come here himself, instead of sending his ruffians in the middle of the night."

One of the soldiers sniggers as Liran sheaths his sword and steps forward. "I send no one to do my work for me. I'm here."

Caril blanches and falls to his knees at the same moment the realization hits Orsiana. In the warm candlelight, it's obvious who the tall, golden-haired captain is.

"Your Majesty," Caril says, "I would have opened the gates had I known you'd arrived."

"I'm sure," the king says. "But I was in a hurry. I've had some worrying news from Abia."

"Nothing to worry about, sire." Even on his knees, Caril is suave. "There's just some vile rumours and a handful of irksome rebels, but I have the situation under control."

"Do you?" the king retorts. "Where's Gospa Orsiana, then?"

"I've been looking for her, every man and woman in Abia has, but she hasn't appeared since that terrible night, and I'm afraid she's de—"

"I'm here," Orsiana cuts in. Her voice is soft, but it rings high and clear like a bell in the musky air. All the heads in the room turn to her.

The king lets out a mocking chuckle, a faint, hollow sound. Behind it, Orsiana hears the Goddess of Love laughing. Such a neat ploy, a fearless maid and a brave captain. Bria and Liran, Gospa Orsiana and Amron V. It's like one of those silly comedies performed in town squares, where lovers separated by enemies fail to recognize one another, walking blind through the world until the mistake is revealed and everything ends well. Sparks rise into the air somewhere above them, but there is no time for this nonsense, because Caril gets up, radiating contempt.

"A fine trick, little Orsiana. I hope you're happy with the uprising and bloodshed you've caused."

"Bloodshed?" Orsiana steps towards her father's desk and the soldiers move out of her way. "You performed a coup. You and your sons and the five treacherous councillors murdered my father in the garden of your villa."

"Is it a crime to remove an incompetent ruler before he destroys the city?" Caril shoots back. "My brother was losing his grip and his mind, and you were a clueless child. Abia was without a ruler."

"But the Great Council and the guilds took care—"

"Don't be a fool," he snarls. "If you let them govern themselves, soon they will realize they don't need you at all. Ask the king if you don't trust me."

Orsiana shoots a glance to Amron V, who shows no intention of joining in. Taking a deep breath, reining in her anger, she asks, "And what was your plan, Uncle? To rule as a tyrant, grab this city by its neck, and bleed it dry?"

"A tyrant? Me?" Caril laughs. "You forget I'm Abian, just like you. We bicker and plot and occasionally assassinate, but we always reach a deal in the end. Had you agreed to my terms of peaceful exile, Abia would've been happy and prosperous. But no, you had to rebel. And for what?"

For what, indeed? The soldiers behind Orsiana shuffle as a cry from the courtyard rises into the night sky. The king crosses his arms, a faint glow of amused disbelief illuminating his handsome face. Outside, oblivious to the drama in the palace, a drunkard sings a love song out of tune. Abia shifts in its sleep, a disturbed, restless city, waiting for good news.

"I did it for Abia," Orsiana says. "To save it from you and your corrupt friends."

"You should've let the city deal with its own problems.

We're like alley cats, fighting over a barrel of fish. You set a lion upon us." Caril's self-assurance is back in the saddle as he looks at the king. "The Council won't be happy when they hear of this nightly breach. This is a gross abuse of the royal power. No king after Amris has ever entered Abia with blades drawn, ready to disrupt the laws and customs of the city."

Orsiana sucks in an angry breath, ready to lash out at her uncle for the audacity to play the injured side, his hands covered in blood up to his elbows, but the king is faster.

"I'll be the first one, then." He keeps his arms crossed, as if he were just an accidental bystander in this scene. "I've heard enough. As soon as my men catch the other conspirators, there will be a trial in the courtyard. No need for the Council, the matter is fairly simple." A faint, icy smile lifts a corner of his mouth. "The sentence will be carried out at dawn."

Every nobleman has the right to be judged by his peers, and Caril, as the nominal ruler of the city—even under the highly dubious circumstances—has the right to a hearing before the Great Council. The king has absolutely no right to mete out justice in Abia.

Caril lets out an incoherent growl while Orsiana cries, "You can't do that!"

"You will find out that I can," the king says, motioning at his men to take Caril away.

As they drag him past Orsiana, Caril hisses, "If you think this is good for you or for Abia, you're fooling yourself."

A cold droplet of fear slides down Orsiana's neck. These are the bitter words of a loser, but by now she's learnt to hear the echo of prophesy, and it rings clear and true in his words.

She waits until the soldiers leave her father's study and then grabs the king's arm before he can follow them. "Please," she says. "You promised no more bloodshed."

He pauses in mid-stride. "This is justice, not bloodshed."

"But the Council and the city will see this as an attack on

their freedom. Caril must be punished, but they should be the ones punishing him." She tries to reason with him, clinging to his arm, wishing she was bigger, capable of radiating the energy of a predator, not a fussy bird.

He pulls himself out of her grasp lightly, detaching her without effort, but as his bare skin touches hers, a surge of unnatural warmth flashes through her body. They both gasp as they draw apart. Her heart skips a beat, her stomach twists. He blushes and clears his throat.

"This idea of self-governing, of the special status, is outdated." The words cross his lips with some effort, his eyes clouded, the political history fished out with a hook. "Amris conceded because he had bigger problems, because he had to move fast and lay siege to Syr. But that was three hundred years ago, and Abia is just as quarrelsome and arrogant as it has always been. This is an ideal opportunity to change that."

Orsiana steps back in horror. Her mouth is dry, but still she manages to ask, "And do what?"

"Rule it from Amraith, like every other city in the kingdom." He rubs his neck and loosens the collar of his shirt, looking flustered and struggling to continue. "You will keep the title and the Council will remain in place if they bow their heads, but the important decisions will be made by me."

"I'd sooner die than let you do that," she says, bewildered and reckless.

Beneath their conflict there's something else, though, something perilous and enthralling. Orsiana's agitated mind cannot decide if she *likes* the king, his manner, his views. She finds him quite infuriating, to tell the truth. And yet, she cannot tear her eyes away from his face. And he's under the same spell, she realizes, staring at her like a starving street urchin stares at a cake.

The Goddess of Love and her tricks and deceptions. Orsiana cannot bear to stand close to this man, she cannot—

Without a word, he scoops her up in his arms, bends down— a shadow blocking the light—and kisses her. His lips are soft and it starts lightly, but it grows more intense as their tongues meet. Orsiana, who has never been kissed like that, never been kissed properly at all, closes her eyes, feeling the heat of his body radiating through the layers of clothing as her sparse flesh grinds against his hard muscles. A wave of desire rises in her belly and surges between her thighs, a hundred times stronger than the gentle longing she felt daydreaming about Mareo. She thrusts her hips towards him, not sure what she wants, but adamant that she wants it right now. He responds, pushing her to the desk, lifting her skirts. His weight presses her down and his hand clears the clutter beneath her with an impatient swipe, poorly, because as soon as she lies down, something stabs her in the back.

The pain is immediate and sobering. It shatters the glamour and as a muffled cry escapes her lips, she realizes what she has got herself into. The king is strong but Orsiana is slippery, and she wriggles out of his grasp like an eel, putting some distance between their bodies.

He's slow on the uptake, his eyes glazed, his face flushed with desire. His confusion lasts only a heartbeat, and then the sharp smile of a predator lights up his face. He thinks she's playing a game.

She has nowhere to run. "Stop, please," she says, her back against the wall. "You're scaring me."

To his credit, he does stop. His laughter is a rusty blade dragged over a whetstone as he rubs his eyes, removing the cobwebs of glamour, and says, "Run away then, my lady, and let me finish what I started."

She flees her father's study without looking back.

~

ORSIANA RUNS into the first empty room, her father's bedchamber, and falls to her knees on the carpet, cursing the gods. Korab and Veles goaded her with their tricks, Lada cleared her path and greased it until it's so slippery there's nothing to hold on to and pause. She slides towards her destiny, gaining speed, a helpless toy in their hands. It confirms her belief that they have never been on her side, not really, despite the otherworldly magic wrapping her in its gauzy veils. All those miracles; they don't serve her, they serve the king. Abia will fall like a ripe plum into his hands.

The king.

It's not love, it can't be love. Love is supposed to be gentle and deep and long-lasting, not this searing lust, these claws that rake her from the inside. It must be one of Lada's tricks; it overrides her reason with no regard for decency or common sense. She's like a filly in heat, stomping around, foaming at her mouth. And yet, and yet ... all those sensual poems and obscene illustrations, they reflected the truth of it. Oh, how Mistress Divna would laugh if she could see her now. And her father ...

He would laugh too at his naïve child, at his headstrong, baffled daughter.

"Oh Father," she whispers, "what am I going to do?"

Moon sails over the night sky and Orsiana berates herself as the truth of her father's death sinks in with undeniable finality. It's not just that he's gone now, it's that he's gone forever. Every moment in her life from now on, every joy and sadness, every major decision or minor disappointment Orsiana will face without him. She is alone in the world, and she doesn't know what to do.

A weight-driven musical clock whirrs and plays its tune, reminding her that the summer night is short. Before the melody ends, Orsiana is already on her feet, wiping her tears. The king has posted his guards on the main entrances to the palace, but this is her home and he has no right to tell her what to do. She sneaks out like a tiny mouse, and runs into the sleeping city.

Five councillors conspired with Caril to overthrow her father and Orsiana knows the king's men will drag them to the palace tonight. Serves them right; they should feel at least a fraction of the horror and despair they caused her. The remaining seven, however, the ones peacefully sleeping in their beds, unaware of the turmoil in the palace—they're the ones Orsiana needs.

She runs to Councillor Zentio's house first, not because it's the nearest one, but because she is certain the old man hates Caril. This is not the time to bother with back entrances and secret corridors; she bangs on the door, shouting, "Open in the name of Lady Orsiana."

A sleepy servant unlocks the door, pushes his head through the narrow crack, and gapes at her, mouth open like a stunned frog.

"Yes, it's me." Orsiana shoves him aside and marches in. "Wake your master, tell him it's important and extremely urgent."

Orsiana is shown to Councillor Zentio's study and the old man shows up before she manages to grind her teeth to dust, followed by a maid carrying a pot of fresh tea and honey cakes.

"Is it really you, my lady?" he asks.

"Who else?" She allows him a grandfatherly kiss on the cheek and a careful hug. His bones creak under the layers of fine linen and wool, and he smells of parchment and dust. "I'll explain it all. But first, you must send a message to the councillors to gather here immediately. The king is in Abia and he'll have Caril executed at dawn if we don't stop him."

Councillor Zentio blinks and she can almost see the questions swarming in his head. The Great Council has never acted in haste; it is the middle of the night, there is no precedent.

"I hate my uncle more than you do," Orsiana says. "But this is not about him."

The old councillor nods and sends the messengers while Orsiana polishes off honey cakes like a hungry squirrel.

"Will you tell me what happened to you while we wait?"

She nods, her mouth full, but once she swallows the cake, she realizes there isn't much she can say without appearing crazy. Korab and drowning, Veles and his shapeshifting, dying and being risen by the Goddess of Love—it's all the stuff of legends and folk tales, best kept hidden. In the end, she shares the only useful thing. "I commissioned Mareo to write the ballad. Every word is true."

"I thought as much. I am so sorry for your loss." Tears fill his rheumy eyes and he wipes them with a crumpled handkerchief. "I remember your father as a young man. Burning with energy, shining with joy, full of plans and dreams and ideas. And then—"

"And then." Orsiana closes the subject, afraid that here, in this friendly study, smaller than her father's but just as cluttered, a new wave of grief might drown her, render her incapable of carrying on.

Fortunately, the councillors appear, one by one, rubbing their eyes and yawning. Councillor Darizio, the youngest of them, is the last to walk in, gaudily dressed, trailing a cloud of alcohol fumes that reveal he hasn't been sleeping. "What's this all about, then?" he asks. "Are the remaining five coming?"

"No," Orsiana says. "They conspired with Caril to kill my father, and they will be dealt with in due time." In the silence that follows, she stands up and lifts her head. She is short and dressed as a maid and young enough to be a granddaughter to most of them, and she cannot keep her voice from shaking. "The king has entered Abia tonight with his guard and seized the palace. He sentenced Caril and his accomplices to death without a trial. As my father's only true heir, I ask you to help me stop the king from executing Caril at dawn and effectively taking Abia."

"The king is here?" Surprised murmurs, questions, demands for explanation fill the room.

"His soldiers entered Abia?"

"Who let him in?"

"My lords, we have no time," Orsiana reminds them.

"Why should we save Caril just to sentence him to death ourselves?" Councillor Renzo raises his voice above the commotion. "Let the king do it and exonerate us from having Caril's blood on our hands. He still has many friends in this town."

A few heads nod, but Councillor Zentio opposes him. "If we let the king do this, it means we accept his will is above our own. If we let him rule now, we let him rule forever."

"Who else should rule us, then?" Councillor Renzo shoots back.

"My lords," Orsiana pleads, "you know my claim is true and I am my father's sole remaining heir. But we can discuss it all later—"

"You're too young," a voice cuts in.

In the sudden silence that follows, Orsiana searches their faces. She doesn't know who said it, but she can see them measuring her up, comparing her to Gospodar Orsolo and finding her lacking.

Councillor Darizio clears his throat. "Your claim is legitimate, my lady," he says, "but—"

"You're only eighteen, you need a mentor, a guardian."

"And you have no family left. Caril has disgraced himself, and now you have no close male relatives."

"I didn't need any male relatives to survive Caril's coup," she retorts.

They refuse to meet her eyes, clearly uncomfortable that she dares to oppose them instead of obeying instantly.

She pushes on, barely swallowing the rising frustration. "And eighteen is old enough to rule, you know the law as well as I do. My great-grandfather was eighteen when—"

"He was a man," Councillor Darizio interrupts her.

She is dumbstruck for a heartbeat, completely lost for words. Then anger flares up in her chest, and with it comes the voice. "Is this really what you're going to do now? Discuss my right to rule Abia? While my uncle and his sons and five members of this very Council are dragged to their execution in the courtyard of the palace? While the king is getting ready to seize the power in the city? *Is this what you're going to do now, my lords?*"

Her voice rises to a shriek. She sees her reflection in their eyes: a screaming, dishevelled, unreasonable girl, and she knows she has lost them even before Councillor Morin says, "There's no need to be rash."

"We'll send our men to negotiate with the king."

"He won't dare to do it without consulting us."

Swallowing a scream, Orsiana meets Councillor Zentio's eyes. The old man shrugs with a faint smile and Orsiana remembers that The Great Council has never, ever, made a quick, unanimous decision in the whole written history of Abia.

What were the king's words? *Quarrelsome and arrogant.*

She turns on her heel and marches out and they don't even notice she's gone.

ORSIANA THINKS she'll have to do it all alone, again, but when she steps out of Councillor Zentio's house, there is a small crowd gathered in the street. The messengers carried Councillor Zentio's call to the other councillors' houses, and the servants overheard the news, and whispered among themselves. The whispers spread, and now there is almost three dozen people before the main entrance, even though it's the middle of the night.

"That's just some serving girl," someone mutters.

"No, you fool," a woman retorts, "I've seen her a hundred times, walking with her father. It's her."

Orsiana pauses at the top of the stairs, realizing everybody is looking at her.

"It's her," another woman says. "It's Gospa Orsiana."

For the first time in her life, Orsiana cannot hide behind her father. The people wait—for what, she has no idea. Her feet itch with the impulse to flee, but if she runs now, she might as well keep on running. All the power she wrestles back from Caril, the Council, and the king will be useless if she cannot face the citizens of Abia.

Orsiana is not a marble statue or a doll, but she is the true heiress to Abia. So she pulls herself up and says, "It's me. I'm alive and well and I'm going to the palace to take back what is mine." In a moment of wild inspiration, she adds, "Spread the word. Tell everybody to come to the main entrance, at dawn."

And then she runs, as if chased by a pack of wild dogs.

She reaches the palace as the sky above changes from black to dark purple. The sharp sea wind carries the scent of salt and spices from the docks. Sconces on the walls glow deep orange, their light dwindling at the night's end. Orsiana slips in the same way she got out, and scurrying up the secret stairs, out of the view of the king's men, reaches her bedroom.

There is no time to call the maids, to draw a bath, do her hair or don her jewels, but she'll be damned if she appears in the courtyard dressed as a scullery maid. There is only so far she can go in a tattered smock.

She rummages through her chests and pulls the first fine things she touches: a soft linen shift, a heavy satin gown, lapis blue with silver embroidery. She finds a pitcher filled with stale water and uses a rag to scrub the grime off her skin. She brushes her hair in a dozen firm strokes—whatever Lada did with it left it heavy and silken and for the first time in her life, a braid doesn't fall apart in Orsiana's hands before she can tie the end. She puts on the fine clothes just as the first trace of light appears in the east.

By the time she descends to the main courtyard, the torches are paler than tired glow worms against the background of the dawn sky. The sea wind is at its sharpest now, slicing like a butcher's knife through her clothes. Orsiana shivers, hidden behind a massive column near the main gate, and waits.

Sunlight pours on the roofs of the palace like liquid fire; a flock of sparrows darts across the cloudless sky. Someone barks an order in the dark passage on the opposite side to the main gate and the king steps out of the shadow, followed by his men leading Caril, his sons, and the five treacherous councillors, hands tied behind their backs. The prisoners stagger and hesitate, turning their heads in disbelief. Caril's twin boys sport bruises on their cheeks and blood on their shirts; one of the councillors still wears a nightshirt, hastily tucked into breeches.

The last time Orsiana saw them together, they were stabbing her father like murderous beasts, their faces inhuman in the flickering light, their eyes manic, pitiless. A part of her would rejoice at seeing their heads chopped off here in the yard. It would be so easy to let the king murder them: it would feed the ravenous, grieving darkness inside her. But then their blood would be on her hands and she could never wash it off.

"On your knees!" The guards push the prisoners down.

There is no wooden block, no masked executioner, and for a moment, Orsiana doesn't understand how the king plans to kill them. A sharp sound cuts the silence, a sword being pulled out of the scabbard, and one of the soldiers approaches with a long blade in his hands.

The king is dressed the same as his guards, in dark wool, his golden hair tied with a leather strap. He seems disinterested, almost distracted, as the men kneel before him. One of the councillors sobs softly, Orsiana's cousins draw close, and Caril stares straight ahead, refusing to acknowledge the king's presence.

Sunlight pours down the red roof tiles and touches the gleaming white stone of the walls. The king paces, making a few quick turns, and then stops.

"You have betrayed your lord," the king says. "You conspired to overthrow him, you set a trap and murdered him in cold blood to grab the power in Abia." He pauses, as if waiting for the condemned men to object, but they remain silent. "The punishment for your crimes is death, according to your own laws and the laws of this kingdom, and I'll have it carried out before I leave." He looks around the silent courtyard. "Do you have anything to say?"

Caril lifts his head. "You have no right to do this," he says. "We deserve a proper trial."

Orsiana grinds her teeth in the shadow. The battle for Abia is being fought right here, in this windblown courtyard, while the councillors squabble over minor details in Councillor Zentio's warm study. She hopes against hope they come to their senses and decide to act.

As if sensing Orsiana's thoughts, the king waits for someone else to speak, but no one does. The councillors fail to appear. The silence stretches while sunlight fills the courtyard. At last, the king motions at the soldier with the sword and says, "If that's all—"

Orsiana stares at the scene transfixed: it plays out before her eyes like a vulgar tragedy. She's just a spectator, there's no cue for her to enter. A ray of sunshine reflecting off the long blade wakes her from the trance: a few heartbeats longer and the conspirators will be dead.

She has no real plan, no script, just an inexplicable connection with the city beneath her feet, with Abia nestled in her heart, flowing through her veins. She cannot stop the king alone, he won't listen to her. The gods won't help her. The councillors won't help her. But the city might.

The main gates of the palace are massive things, built of oak and iron, as tall as two men. She could never push them open by herself and it's good that she doesn't have to, because there is a mechanism hidden behind a wooden panel in the wall. The king doesn't know about it, or doesn't care; there's no one guarding it. Orsiana pulls the lever and the doors move soundlessly on well-oiled hinges, perfectly balanced. The light rushes in, the sea wind on its heels.

The executioner's blade stops in mid-air, the king turns his head, someone says, "What—" The people in the courtyard freeze into a tableau.

Orsiana steps into the luminous haze pouring through the door and looks out to the square. There, in perfect, uncanny silence, a thousand people return her gaze. Abia has heard her call. Orsiana trips, her gown suddenly too long for her legs. She feels small before this ocean of people, one tiny drop among the many. There's no point in clutching the idea of herself so tightly; Orsiana is Abia and Abia is Orsiana, and they are water, impossible to catch, impossible to crush.

Something extraordinary happens at that moment. Every single heartbeat in the crowd echoes in Orsiana's chest. She hears them inside her, like waves in a half-submerged cave, rhythmic, endless, and what they radiate towards her is love.

Lada may have promised her love, but Abia delivered it.

Orsiana falls to her knees on the flagstones. The square is warm beneath her hands, pulsating like a live thing. The heart of Abia beats for her.

She presses her forehead to the stone. "Oh you capricious, glorious creature," she whispers. "Help me save you. Help me save myself."

"Orsiana!" someone shouts.

"Orsiana!" another echoes.

Her name rises like a tide from a thousand mouths, lifting her up to her feet again. She spreads her arms wide, closes her eyes, surrenders herself. The exhilaration is intoxicating.

At that instant, the roar turns into a scream. Orsiana doesn't see the man, only feels the hand pulling her back and the hot kiss of the blade sliding between her ribs.

THE DARKNESS SUCKS HER IN; slices off the sound, the light, the warmth.

"They all want you, my brothers and sisters," a voice says. "But I was faster."

Orsiana's eyes adjust to the sluggish, shifting streaks of light emanating from an invisible source far above. She seems to be in an endless chamber with massive columns rising up, strong enough to hold the sky.

She blinks and there is a woman standing before her, dressed in dark grey and green, with long tresses of black hair writhing around her head in the perfectly still air.

"You took something that belongs to me," the Goddess of Death says.

It's such a preposterous claim that Orsiana's throat releases a rattle-like laughter as she falls to her knees. Every person she loved is dead: her mother, her brothers, her father. Even Mareo, with his lofty words and lowly ways. Death took them all.

"You like feeling sorry for yourself, don't you?" the

Goddess says. "But you know well who I mean. The condemned men."

"Their destiny was yet undecided," Orsiana protests very softly.

"Wrong."

Can one argue with a deity? *This* deity? "Are you going to take me instead?"

"It depends," the Goddess says. "What do you want?"

On her knees, Orsiana stares at the monochrome mosaic depicting waves on the floor and for the first time thinks of a true wish. "I want to finish what I started in Abia."

The Goddess glides closer. "And what are you willing to pay for it?" The coils of her hair move towards Orsiana, like snakes studying their prey.

Orsiana is familiar with this divine game. "You want them, don't you? The eight heads rolling in the courtyard?"

"You think this is unfair?"

Orsiana should be afraid, she should be terrified arguing with Morana. But fear has slunk into some dark hole, dragging anger with it. Orsiana's chest is filled with resignation. "There's a lesson in it, right?"

The Goddess of Death doesn't laugh or tease or threaten. She merely nods.

"And the lesson is ..." Orsiana frowns. "I can't save everyone?"

"No. The lesson is there will be blood on your hands no matter what you do. You survive, they die. You die, the crowd tears them apart, dozens die. Heads rolling in any case." The Goddess cocks her head, looks at Orsiana with her bottomless eyes. "Do you think your father never signed a death warrant? You know your future husband has. Every ruler has. That's the nature of the job. If you can't do it, it's better for you to give up now."

The weight of Morana's words is crushing, but the

goddess is not done with her yet. She kneels down beside Orsiana, filling her nostrils with the odour of decay.

"There's so much death ahead of you, little Orsiana. You think you've lost much? One day you'll know what it feels like to lose everything."

"I don't want a deal with you."

"I don't care. Because wherever you go, I will be right behind you. You will see my reflection in a still water of a pond, my shadow in the corner of your room on a sleepless night, the glint of my sickle in your children's eyes."

"No!"

"No!"

"Orsiana? Orsiana? Look at me!"

The first thing she sees is his pale, frightened face. He holds her in his arms, pressing the spot where the blade went in.

She breathes in and her lungs expand without collapsing. Her ribs burn, though.

"Wait, let me see," she says.

The king moves his hand a fraction, his palm covered in blood. Her dress is torn and so is her skin, but it's just a flesh wound.

Her ears are ringing, but that's not where the sound comes from. The palace courtyard is filled with a deafening roar of an angry beast.

Orsiana struggles to remember. The square, the crowd, the execution. On her left, behind the king, two guards hold down her cousin while he hisses like a wild cat. A bloody pocket knife lies on the flags beside him. The gates of the palace are closed. Outside, the fury of the mob grows like a winter storm.

"Why did you close the gates?"

"They surged forward when you fell. They would've torn us all to pieces," the king says.

"Help me get up," she orders. He lifts her easily and offers his hand for support. She steps away, her legs shaky, her body not quite her own. "Open the gates."

"Orsiana—"

"Open the gates!"

He turns to his guards and nods. One of them pulls the lever.

"May the gods help us," the king says.

Like a flood breaking the dam, the crowd pours in. Orsiana shivers, sick with fear, yet she stands firm. She doesn't need the gods, she doesn't need the king. All she needs is her city to feel her. She opens her arms.

And the tide stops.

People are still crowding in, pushing forward, but there's an invisible line before Orsiana they do not cross. They fill the courtyard, eyeing her bloody dress, her cousin on the ground, the seven condemned men waiting for their destiny.

It's time for retribution; she cannot escape it, she must give them closure, otherwise they'll take justice in their own hands.

Turning towards the guards, she orders, "Bring the prisoners forth."

The remaining seven men are dragged in front of her. Caril looks at the knife on the ground and then at Orsiana, shrugging with derision.

She pulls herself up, ignoring the pain.

"Just say the word and you'll have their heads," the king whispers in her ear.

His words echo in the endless chamber filled with shifting darkness.

The courtyard is packed now, the mob surrounding them

in a tight circle. All eyes on her, and silence so perfect you could hear a pin drop.

"You murdered my father in cold blood," she tells the conspirators. "You deserve to die, and death is what I'll give you." She pauses. The executioner lifts his sword, waiting for her order. She shakes her head. "I won't have you executed, though. Abia has seen enough blood. No, your death will be different." She takes a few moments to study their faces, to take in every line and shadow. Caril, always quick on the uptake, blanches. He's already portrayed himself as a martyr, but Orsiana won't give him that pleasure. "I banish you forever, pronounce you dead in the eyes of the law. You are not citizens of Abia anymore; your names will be erased from the records, your property forfeited, your children sent to foster families far away from here. I'll dismantle every memory of you, erase every deed. It won't be like you died, it'll be like you've never lived at all." She doesn't give them a chance to reply. In the perfect silence, she turns to the guards and says, "Take these bodies to the harbour and put them on the first ship that sails out on the morning tide."

No one protests, no one questions her decision. The guards seize the stunned men and drag them out of the court-yard. Caril looks over his shoulder and opens his mouth, but Orsiana gently shakes her head and smiles, erasing his words from existence. The crowd opens before the eerie procession, forming a straight path across the square. She follows them with her eyes until they're nothing but insignificant dots, and then the path closes and the crowd swallows the last trace of them.

Orsiana and the king remain alone in the circle, bathed in the golden sunlight.

"Go home, it's over," Orsiana says, to the crowd, to the king, to herself.

Nobody moves.

"I think they need one more thing," the king says softly, taking her hand. He cuts a fine figure, tall and dashing, as he draws her close and locks her in an embrace. The silence lingers for a heartbeat more.

Then he bends down and kisses her and the crowd erupts in cheers.

~

SHE SHOULD BE ANGRY, Orsiana thinks a few hours later, watching the empty courtyard through the window and pulling at the bandage wrapped tight around her ribcage. Her heart surprises her with relief and mild amusement instead.

The king is no fool. In fact, he outsmarted them all, Orsiana and the crowd. He gave them the one thing more interesting than blood and revenge: the illusion of a happy ending.

Orsiana lifts her hand to her mouth and touches her lips, remembering the kiss and basking in the echo of its sweetness. She discussed husbands with her father, one dark winter afternoon when she turned eighteen, a lifetime ago. He had a list on his desk, along with a pile of letters filled with promises and reeking of self-interest.

"There is just one logical choice for an heiress as important as you are," he told her then. "Everything else will obstruct the balance of power." He crammed the list and the letters into an overflowing drawer. "He has asked for your hand and I promised I'd consider it. But I'm selfish and I'm not ready to let go of you just yet."

Orsiana sighs, basking in the sunlight on a bench by the window, soothed by the gentle rhythm of the waves rolling in the distance. The time for procrastination is up. There is a knock on the door and a little page opens it, announcing, "His Royal Highness, Amron V."

His nonchalant good looks are disturbing, his calculating eyes even more so. She tricked him into thinking she was a humble maid; he tricked her into believing he was a mere captain of the guard. He stole her power trying to execute Caril; she took it back rousing the city. He kissed her in public, sealing a relationship that didn't exist; she forced him to face the Council afterwards and ask for their blessing.

They're quite a good match, apparently.

"The Council agreed," he says. "Reluctantly."

Orsiana reminds herself she should be above gloating, but she indulges for just a little while. The king brought the Council to heel. He gave them back their illusion of power, but he took Orsiana. And they couldn't complain, because it was them who demanded she should find someone older—a man—to guide her. The king is barely over twenty, but that's easy to forget when the full weight of his brief, intense attention falls on you.

"I'm sure there's a draft of our wedding contract somewhere in my father's archive," she says. "He would've prepared for it well in advance."

The king sits beside her on the bench. The seat is narrow; he is careful not to touch her but she cannot escape the salty scent of his hair, the warmth of his body, a finger's breadth from hers. He rests his hands on his knees; she notices he wears no jewellery, not even a signet ring. "Are sure you want to do it?" he asks. A shadow of a smile reveals he's not entirely serious.

She's heard the rumours. And even if she hadn't, one look at the blushing maids throwing themselves in his path tells her enough. He is a wildfire and the world is his fuel. He wants it all: power, conflict, girls, glory.

Orsiana is made of water, though. Salty spray carried by the winter gales and black, undisturbed depths where white bones of the long-dead sailors find eternal rest. She will handle it. It's the price she must pay for Abia.

"I want you to promise me one thing," she says, putting her left hand on his right. No magic sparks between them; her encounter with Morana burnt Lada's glamour to ashes. Still, the warmth of his skin is comforting. "Abia remains the same as it is, mine to rule and mine to leave to whomever I want."

Her pride cringes at this begging, but her reason sees that Abia, herself, and the king now form a triangle. Abia needs Orsiana to restore the peace and secure its rights, to protect it from the king's greed. Orsiana needs the king to back her rule and keep the Council at bay. The king needs Abia to bend the knee to show his strength, to use it as an example for other would-be usurpers. They stand in perfect balance: if one of them breaks, they all break.

"They don't really love you, you know." He regards her with a dark blue gaze of pragmatism. "They love the image of you: young, pretty, and tragic."

For the briefest of moments, his golden mask falls down and she sees the man behind it: overburdened, alone, with all eyes on him all the time. A blink and it's gone.

"I know," she says, "but I love them just the same. Do you promise?"

"You have my word."

"And we'll put it in the marriage contract?"

His smile is a curved blade. "You don't trust me, do you?"

"Why should I?"

But then she twists her shoulders a little, moves closer to him. He turns his head so that his mouth hovers just above hers. She closes the remaining gap with excruciating slowness, drinking in his warmth, until their lips meet in a butterfly caress.

～

GOSPODAR ORSOLO'S body is found in the cellar of the palace, wrapped in linen and packed in ice. Orsiana has it embalmed and displayed for three days in the great hall, so that the people of Abia can say their goodbyes. Then, in a long, magnificent ceremony, she escorts him to the family crypt and lays him beside her mother and brothers. She has no family left now, but seeing them together is a consolation. As long as they are resting in peace, she can face the world. And she is not alone anymore: the king stands beside her, his arm wrapped around her shoulders.

Mareo's body is found in a mass grave, exhumed and buried in another solemn public ceremony. Orsiana commissions a collection of his poems to be printed by Mistress Divna, a beautiful, leather-bound, illustrated tome. It's bitter consolation, a paltry payment for the young poet's life.

Mistress Divna, however, tells her, "That's the best memento any of us can hope for." Then she hugs Orsiana and whispers in her ear, "I wish you all the happiness in the world. Your father would be proud of you."

They both cry in her little office at the end of Kissing Alley.

ON THE MORNING of her wedding day, Orsiana offers gifts to the gods. White flowers and scented oil scattered upon the waves for Korab. Gold dust and incense poured into the dark crevice on a craggy hill for Veles. And two white doves trailing red ribbons for Lada. She prays to them, but quietly, hoping her words will never reach their ears again.

The fourth goddess gets nothing because all the gifts in the world fall into her hands, eventually, and turn to dust.

Orsiana and Amron V say their vows on the main square, on a wooden dais raised in its centre, before the eyes of the whole city. He doesn't begrudge her the wedding contract, more interested in her person than her dowry. But it's only temporary, Orsiana knows, and when it passes, she will have to fight for every right written down in that document. He's a hard man, her husband, and as fickle as the gods.

None of this matters to her, though. Her gaze slips away from his face and flies over the crowd—taking in the palace, the houses with their red roofs, the harbour with the ships rocking gently—and a surge of love fills her chest. No king, no gods will ever take this from her, and no price will ever be too high to pay for it. She is Abia, every street and square, every garden and house, every man, woman and child; it's all built into her bones and flesh, a part of her forever. Her city, her heart.

ACKNOWLEDGMENTS

This novella started as a short story, a fun little prequel about Orsiana that sat at the back of my mind and nagged me to write it down. I thought – five or six thousand words should do it. Reader, I was wrong. Typically, I'm an underwriter, but this story just grew and grew until it turned into a proper novella and left me with the problem of doing something about it.

It was incredibly handy that my favourite writing community, Codex, held their annual Novella Contest at that time. I'm incredibly grateful to my fellow Codexians from Pinky and Brain divisions who read it first and offered me their valuable insights. Their suggestions made this story much better.

I'm grateful to all the writers and editors who supported me on my writing journey, who read and loved my debut. Without their friendship, I'd never have the courage to write the next thing. Thank you, Genoveva Dimova, Kate Heartfield, Lucy Holland, Jess Hyslop and Ai Jiang for your kind words on *Dark Woods, Deep Water*. I also found unexpected and warm support at home, from reviewers, podcasters and journalists. Thank you, *Morina kutija*, Katarina Podobnik, Kristian Sirotich and Edi Prodan.

My editor Ed Crocker not only made this story better, but also made me laugh in the process, which is no small feat. My publisher Antonia Rachel Ward is a great professional and a true friend. I'm grateful to the whole Ghost Orchid team. Also, warmest thanks to the artists who brought my characters to life, Mia Minnis and Dory Whynot. All books should be illustrated (by human artists)!

Lastly, my family still stick up for me on this crazy journey, even if it steals all my free time and brings me virtually no money. My parents support me, my husband celebrates every victory with me and my teen daughter is not half as ashamed with me as she has every right to be. My cat is bloody useless, but I love her nevertheless.

Jelena Dunato
June 2024

ABOUT THE AUTHOR

Jelena Dunato is an art historian, curator, speculative fiction writer and lover of all things ancient. She grew up in Croatia on a steady diet of adventure novels and then wandered the world for a decade, building a career in the arts.

Jelena's stories have been published in *Beneath Ceaseless Skies, The Dark, Future SF and Mermaids Monthly*, among others. She is a member of SFWA and Codex.

Jelena lives on an island in the Adriatic with her husband, daughter and cat.

You can find Jelena on her website jelenadunato.com or on social media as @jelenawrites (X, BlueSky) and jelena_author (Instagram).

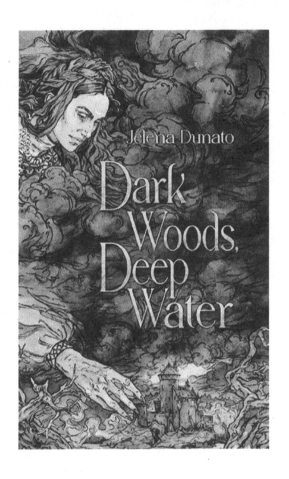

ghostorchidpress.com

Milton Keynes UK
Ingram Content Group UK Ltd.
UKHW040725270924
448919UK00004B/135